COLD CALLS

Also by Charles Benoit

Relative Danger

Out of Order

Noble Lies

You

Fall from Grace

COLD

CHARLES

CLARION BOOKS

CALLS

BENOIT

Houghton Mifflin Harcourt | Boston New York

CLARION BOOKS

215 Park Avenue South

New York, New York 10003

Clarion Books is an imprint of Houghton Mifflin
Harcourt Publishing Company.

www.hmhbooks.com

The text was set in Chaparral Pro.
Design by Sharismar Rodriguez

Library of Congress Cataloging-in-Publication Data
Benoit, Charles.
Cold calls / Charles Benoit.
pages cm
Summary: While on suspension, Shelly, Eric, and Fatima, who have
nothing else in common, try to identify and stop the person who
blackmailed each of them by phone to perform very specific acts
of bullying at their high schools.
ISBN 978-0-544-23950-0 (hardcover)
[1. Extortion — Fiction. 2. Bullying — Fiction. 3. Revenge — Fiction.
4. High schools — Fiction. 5. Schools — Fiction. 6. Mystery and
detective stories.] I. Title.
PZ7.B447114Col 2014
[Fic] — dc23
2013016271

Manufactured in the United States of America
DOC 10 9 8 7 6 5 4 3 2 1
4500457880

It's no secret, it's all for Rose.

ONE

THE PHONE RANG AND HE ANSWERED IT.

Later, when it looked like it was over, he'd think back on that moment and what he could have done different.

But that was weeks away, and it was just a phone call.

No number came up on caller ID. It was weird, but it happened now and then, somebody calling from a pay phone or using a cheap throwaway. If he had recognized the number — Nick or Duane or Andrew or Yousef or one of the guys from the team — he would have said something that sounded like "'Zup." If it had been Kate or Tabitha or Felicia or Emma or any girl — even April — he would have said, "Hey."

It wouldn't have been April, though. It was still too early to say if they'd even get back to being just friends.

With no number to recognize, he went with "'Zup?"

There was a pause on the other end and the sound of air being sucked through a straw, then two quick clicks, and then a voice, computer generated and pitched low like distant thunder. "Eric Hamilton."

At first he thought it was the library. They had an automated system that called when a book went overdue, and

1

the calls would come around that time in the evening, not so early that it disturbed dinner, not so late that it was rude. But he hadn't been in any library since June. Besides, their message started friendly before getting into the details. There was nothing friendly in this voice.

More clicks, static. "Eric Hamilton."

Somebody screwing around. The stupid kind of thing you did in sixth grade, or the first time you got high. And it wasn't even funny then. He pressed END, tossed the phone onto his bed, and went back to *Gears of War*.

Ten minutes later, the phone buzzed and he answered without thinking.

That hollow air sound, the clicks. "Eric Hamilton."

If he was outside or home alone, he would have rattled off some f-bombs and hung up, but he could hear his mother outside his door, shifting things around in the hall closet, and he didn't talk like that when she could hear him. And maybe it wasn't a prank. Maybe it was some new computerized program telling him there'd be no school tomorrow.

Probably not, but it was worth checking.

"Yeah, this is Eric," he said, then heard himself saying it, a faint echo that swirled out into the airy static.

There was a pause and something that sounded like a breath.

Then a single whispered sentence that made his stomach drop.

Then nothing.

He held the phone tight to his ear, waiting for more, holding it there until three quick beeps told him the call was over.

He sat at the edge of his bed, the phone in his lap, his thumb hovering above the keypad, the caller's whispered words still in his head.

After a minute, he swiped the phone back on and went to the list of recent calls. It showed only one that day — a missed call from his mother around noon. So either he imagined the whole thing or whoever it was knew a few clever phone tricks.

He knew he hadn't imagined the call, but maybe he had imagined what he heard. Or maybe he was just reading too much into the static, making words out of the random sounds, putting them together into that sentence.

Besides, even if he did hear it right, it was the kind of thing you can say to anybody and it would make them nervous.

Eric put the phone on his desk, then pulled a sweatshirt out of the bottom drawer of his dresser. It was a warm night, but still he shivered. He went back to the game, and after a dozen stupid mistakes and restarts in a row, he closed out, set his alarm for six, turned off the light, and stared at the ceiling for an hour until he fell asleep.

The fifth time the buzz sounded, he hit the snooze on his alarm. Then the buzz sounded again, and he realized it was his phone.

One eye open, he lifted his head enough to see the red 2:47 on the clock. He reached for the phone, knocking it off the desk. It fell onto the carpet and under the bed. He listened through his pillow as it buzzed seven more times. It stopped and he waited, picturing the call going to voice mail, then the hang-up and the redial.

It started again, and on the ninth buzz he leaned over the side and fumbled until he found it. The blue light from the screen lit up the dark room, the swoosh of the static roaring in the silence. He was squinting to see the keypad, trying to remember what buttons to push to activate call blocking, when the voice said, "Check your inbox." Then the line went dead and the blue light faded down to a soft glow.

Eric dropped the phone back on the floor and rolled over, wrapping the pillow around his head. He lay like that for fifteen, twenty minutes, not moving, telling himself he was just about to fall asleep, when he gave in, sat up, and tapped on his iPad.

He had opened a Gmail account a couple of years back

but never used it. Everybody was on Facebook or they just sent a text. He needed an email address to put on college applications, and he checked it now and then, but all he got were generic ads and personalized invitations from the army and marines.

It took him three tries to get the password right.

He had a dozen unopened messages — the first several were weeks old, the last one had come in at midnight.

There was nothing in the subject line, and the return email address was a bunch of question marks from an EarthLink account. He clicked it open, and when it loaded, a pasted-in picture filled the screen.

A black rectangle at the top, a rough white area in the middle, a dark brown bar along the bottom.

No people, no words, nothing else in the shot.

Eric rubbed his eyes and leaned in to the screen.

It was obviously a zoomed-in part of a bigger picture, with the squared-off edges and boxy patches of computer pixels. But a picture of what?

The brown part could be leather or wood or paint or dirt.

The black part looked shiny, so maybe it was metal. But then, it could've been the way the camera flashed.

The white space was too rough to be paper and too smooth to be concrete, and not white like milk — more like vanilla ice cream.

Whatever it was, the voice had assumed he would recognize it and would know what it meant.

But he didn't.

Eric studied it until his eyes went heavy, then turned off the screen and crawled back into bed.

Eight hours later, he was sitting in history class, supposedly watching a video on the Electoral College, when it hit him.

He knew the parts in the photo.

He could see how it fit in place, see the other parts the photo didn't show.

The black rectangle was the bottom left corner of a *Maxim* swimsuit-model poster.

The brown bar was the top of a wooden headboard.

The white area was a bedroom wall.

His bedroom wall.

His headboard.

His poster.

It took a minute for it to click, but it came, rolling like a bead of cold sweat down his spine.

Whoever had taken the picture had been in his room.

TWO

WAITING FOR IT WAS THE WORST.

At first, anyway.

Eric knew there'd be another call.

There *had* to be.

You don't go through all that trouble for a few fuzzy calls that nobody else heard. If it was a joke, they'd call again with the you-got-punked slam and the what-an-idiot insults. That was the whole point, the payoff that made it worth the effort.

He'd expected somebody to say something at school, since that's where the big audience would be — the caller walking up behind him, whispering his name like Darth Vader, him jumping or freaking out in front of everybody, somebody posting it online — but it didn't happen. That was a good thing. But it meant that whatever it was going to be, it was still coming.

If any of his friends were in on it, he would have known. They would have been trying too hard to act normal, but they were lousy actors and he would have seen through them as easily as their teachers and parents and the other people they lied to did. Duane would have had that smart-ass grin he got when he knew something you didn't know, and Andrew would have had that nervous laugh that always meant something was up. Tabitha and Wendy and Dana would have rolled their eyes at the stupidity of it all, Tabitha saying "Whatevs" for the hundredth time that day. But Nick would have told him right away. Not because Nick was his best friend or anything, but because Nick would have forgotten it was supposed to be a secret.

Eric checked his Gmail a dozen times before school was out and then a few times after practice, but there was nothing new. The same spam and that one email with the picture.

Back in his room, he held up his iPad, aligning the black rectangle in the image with the corner of the poster, the brown bar with the headboard. Whoever had taken the picture had stood somewhere between the foot of his bed and the closet door, but since it showed only that little part and it was all zoomed in and grainy, he couldn't tell exactly where.

The poster had been up since last winter, when April's brother, Garrett, had sent it from college. His note had said that he found posters of half-naked women to be exploitive and disrespectful. Posters of half-naked men, however, were apparently different, as the walls of Garrett's dorm room could attest. Since Eric had put up the poster, just about everyone he hung with had been in his room at one time or another, if only for a minute. It would take a lot less than that to snap a picture.

Now, *why* they would do it was something different. His friends could be weird like that.

But what if it wasn't a friend?

What if it wasn't anybody he knew?

A stranger.

The house was empty half the day. You could break in, have a look around, take a picture or two, sneak out without anyone knowing, not leaving a single trace. True, when he and his father had gotten locked out over the summer, they'd spent an hour trying to figure a way in before giving up and waiting for his mother to get home, but just because they couldn't do it didn't mean somebody else would have a problem. So, yeah, it could've happened.

Maybe.

The more he thought about it—a burglar breaking into his house to take a picture of his room—the more ridiculous it sounded. Still, the idea wouldn't go away, and when it crept close to the surface he could feel the hairs on his neck twitch.

There were no calls that night and no new emails in the morning.

He'd received a normal number of text messages and forwarded Facebook postings and Tweets, all big news flashes like "Watching Transformers IV," "Going 2 bed," "Should be studying for physics test," and "Eating pizza. YUMMM!!!" He could've sent his own, something like "Waiting for stalker asshole to call back," but that would've gotten his friends asking questions and let the caller know that he had got in his head.

Eric checked his email again on the way to school.

Nothing.

His father was used to him zoning out during the ride, leaving him free to stare out at the road in front of the Bronco. At first, all he could think about was the caller, but there was nothing new to think about, so other things popped in, things like the reading he forgot to do for English, the run he should have gone on that morning, the ambush he had walked into last night playing *Gears of War*, and, eventually, predictably, unavoidably, he thought about April.

Two months ago next Saturday.

He was positive she would remember.

Not the kind of thing you celebrate, not out loud anyway, but still not the kind of thing you forget.

At least, that's what the movies said.

But then, the movies also said it was all fireworks and funky bass guitars, that it'd be wild and there'd be no guilt or embarrassment and definitely no regrets, especially for him. Well, it wasn't the first time that the best parts were all in the previews. He just wondered if there'd ever be a sequel.

"Anybody home?" his father said, tapping him on the shoulder. Eric blinked, and there he was, back in the Bronco, idling in the bus loop in front of the school.

His father laughed. "I was tempted to see how long you'd sit there like that, but people were starting to stare."

"Sorry. I didn't sleep that good last night," Eric said, then cut off questions by adding, "I had this stupid song stuck in my head is all."

"That's what you get for listening to stupid music."

Eric mumbled something about classic rock as he climbed out of the truck.

"Here, take this," his father said, handing him five bucks. "Get yourself a tall black coffee. That'll wake you up."

He beeped twice as he drove off.

Eric checked his phone. Nothing. He checked it between classes and one more time before practice, but somewhere in the middle of wind sprints it slipped to the back of his mind. That night, he had too much homework to catch up on to waste time waiting for an email that might never come, and he fell asleep fast, so deep under, he wouldn't have heard a hundred phones ring. On Friday, he started focusing on not thinking about April, and by the time the weekend was over, the whole mystery-caller photo thing was as forgotten as last year's Super Bowl loser.

But on Monday night when he answered his phone and heard the techno static and the airy whoosh, it all crashed back—the calls, the photo, the whispered words that made his stomach roll. He waited, listening, and then he couldn't wait any longer. "Who is this?"

The caller laughed, the voice autotuned dark, deep and not human. Eric strained to hear through the white noise. He thought for a moment, then said, "No big deal. I got an app that traces calls, so I've got your number now—"

Another laugh.

"Yeah, it won't be so funny when I—"

"Tell me the first three numbers and I'll leave you alone."

The words came as a surprise, and for a second Eric was tempted to guess, but whoever it was had called his bluff, and he had nothing. He lowered his voice in case his mother was nearby, then rattled off a handful of f-bomb insults before hanging up.

It was stupid, yeah, and probably what the caller wanted him to do, but he needed to do something, and what else did he have?

Lying on his bed, Eric gritted his teeth till his jaw muscles burned, mentally beating the crap out of . . . who? It didn't matter—he'd do it, even if it was a senior. But what senior would waste time doing this? No, it was someone in his class. Or one of the freshmen. Phone pranks were more their speed. But it wouldn't be one freshman acting alone, since freshmen didn't do anything alone. No self-confidence and a pack mentality, especially when it came to kid stuff like this. And since it probably was a bunch of freshmen, the last thing he should have done is what he did, lose his temper. They were probably all huddled together, giggling on the other end, finding it *so frickin' hilarious* that they made a junior swear. He tried to remember a time when stuff like that was funny. He couldn't, but the first months of ninth grade sounded about right.

It wouldn't be anyone who played sports. Even the ninth-graders knew that the coaches had zero tolerance for athletes living up to the stereotype. Low grades, disrespecting substitute teachers, that jock swagger—the coaches came down hard. Prank phone calls weren't up there with stuffing some kid in a locker, but it wouldn't be worth the risk of all those extra laps to find out.

He considered the theater gleeks. The calls had the over-the-top drama and cheesy audio effects, plus there was that unwritten, always there, jock-gleek animosity that gave this kind of prank a higher purpose. But it wasn't them. Tryouts were starting for the school musical, and they'd be wrapped tight in their own little dramas, too busy destroying each other to worry about some soccer player.

The voice was altered, so it could be anybody, even the cheerleaders. But it wouldn't be them, since, one, they were part of the athletic department and, two, they were more mature than that. In every way.

Ten minutes later, he was still thinking about the maturity of the cheerleaders when his phone buzzed, no number showing up in the caller ID.

There was only one way to play it now. He had to keep his cool, act like he was in on the joke, that he found it sorta funny in an old-school kind of way, like watching *Teletubbies* at a keg party. The prank would fizzle out, and the calls would stop. And then he'd find out who was behind them and get his revenge. He swiped on his phone.

"Hey, stranger. I was hoping you'd call back."

There was a long, static-filled pause that made Eric smile. "What's the matter, lose your voice? I'm not surprised—you've been sounding a little hoarse. Try some tea with honey."

"I have something you want."

"A new car? A million dollars? I'd take either one."

A deep breath, then the voice hissed. "It's something you'll want returned."

Eric was ready with a comeback when it sank in, the smile melting off his face as he remembered the email and the picture of his room. He jumped up and flicked on a second light, his eyes racing over his desk, the shelves, looking for a gap, a space that shouldn't be there. He pulled out his wallet. Driver's license, school ID, pictures — nothing missing. He jerked open the top drawer of his desk and saw the cards April had given him, the pictures from the sophomore dance, the Dairy Queen gift card his aunt had sent him, his grandfather's dog tags, some movie ticket stubs, an old lighter. He squeezed the phone as he gritted his teeth, the whole stay-cool plan burned away. *"What did you take?"*

"I didn't take anything," the caller said, confidence back in the artificial voice. *"You* took it."

"*I* took it? I don't know what the hell you're talking about. You're the one that broke into my —"

He jumped at three quick knocks on the door. "Eric? Everything okay?"

Phone against his leg, he took a deep, steadying breath. "Yeah, Mom, I'm fine. Just, uh . . . just on the phone is all."

"Okay, well, hold it down," his mother said, then, from down the hall, adding, "and make it quick. It's a school night."

"All right, I'm almost done," Eric shouted back. He put the phone to his ear, expecting the line to be dead, but the wispy static was still there. Enough of this, he thought.

"Don't call me again," he said. "If you do, I'm calling

the cops. I have proof that you broke into my house —"

"You're forgetting something," the caller said.

"Yeah? Like what?"

The static dropped out, making the whispered words loud and clear. "I know your secret."

Eric laughed. "Oh that. Isn't that a line from *Scary Movie 3*? You could at least try to be original. Bye-bye, asshole," he said, his thumb swiping over to end the call, but not before hearing one last raspy line.

"Check your email."

Eric stuffed the phone in his pocket and went down to the kitchen, grabbed a stack of Oreos and a glass of milk, then sat in front of the TV in the living room and pretended to care about the *Monday Night Football* pregame show. He held out until the end of the first quarter before heading up to his room, shutting the door, and powering up his iPad.

There were four new messages. One from a skateboard company, one from the Armed Forces Recruitment Center, one from Fandango, and one from an unknown sender at an EarthLink account. With two quick taps he trashed the message.

A minute later, he sent it back to the inbox and clicked it open.

The picture popped up, and Eric gasped, stumbling

backwards, his hands numb, his legs shaking, as he collapsed on his bed, the iPad thumping onto the floor.

He looked again, but the picture was still there.

"Oh, shit," he said, no one there to see the color drain from his face.

THREE

SHELLY MEYER PULLED HER HAIR BACK BEHIND HER head, scrunching it up, holding it in place with her right hand, using her left to balance as she leaned over and puked into the sink.

Tried to, anyway.

The way her stomach had been acting — the noises, the rolling, the acid burn creeping up her throat — throwing up should have been easy. But no, it wasn't happening. It wasn't that kind of sick.

Someone knew.

Who it was and how they had found out she didn't know.

Yet.

But someone knew. And she had to find them.

She ran the water in the sink, cupping her hands under the faucet, letting the cold wash over her fingers till they were numb. She lowered her face into her hands. Water trickled along the curve of her neck, disappearing down the front of her white cotton shirt. It was good, and for a moment she allowed herself to relax. And then it was time.

She looked at her reflection in the polished metal mirror.

Black eyeliner, thicker than she'd worn it in middle school.

Blue-black lipstick, fainter than she liked, but darker than the dress code allowed.

Coal black hair, straight from the bottle, the more unmanageable the longer it got.

Crazy goth chick cliché in a Catholic-school uniform, the whole look still a bit foreign.

She wiped a paper towel across her face, slung her backpack over her shoulder, and walked out of the third-floor bathroom, looking for her victim.

Classes had been over for an hour, and the only students left were out on the fields or down in the locker room. There were a few straggler teachers, but they wouldn't be a problem. She'd only been at the school for three weeks, but by then it was obvious that the teachers who stuck around after the last bell were in no rush to get home. Nonna Lucia would have called them "ladies of a certain age and standing," meaning over fifty and divorced. With cats. There were two male teachers at the school, and both of them could have fit in with that crowd if they didn't bolt out faster than the students. The ones who did stay usually clustered around the librarian's tiny office, eating grocery-store pastries and drinking instant cappuccinos. They were okay teachers, she guessed, entertaining and not too demanding, but none of them seemed like the kind you could talk to, not like Ms. Moothry or Mr. Becker. But that was another school and another life.

Shelly rounded the corner near the bio lab. The hall was empty.

Heather Herman: 72 Facebook friends, 0 in common. Likes Katy Perry, *The Walking Dead, The Slayer Chronicles, American Idol,* Women's Premier Soccer League, Vancouver, and Moonlight Creamery double-chocolate fudge.

There was no place on Facebook to list the things she hated, but if there was, Shelly figured she'd be on it by now.

Down the west stairs, past the chapel and the room where Mrs. Holland tried to teach religion, the lessons always turning into class discussions about current events and "teen issues," Catholic-school code for sex and drugs. There were the occasional Bible references, but Shelly knew them better than Mrs. Holland did — she'd even corrected Father Caudillo a couple of times when they'd talk after mass, him half joking about her one day becoming a priest.

But that had been before everything had gone wrong.

Shelly thumbed the metal button on the drinking fountain and swirled the warm water around her dry mouth.

She spit it out and did it a second time, then started down the stairwell to the first floor and the side exit.

She knew how it would play out, how it *had* to go, and she could guess what would happen later.

Maybe not tomorrow, but soon.

There'd be the call to the principal's office, a visit to the counselor, then a meeting with her father — good luck with that — then the psychiatrist, maybe a scared-straight talking-to by a priest or a cop or an attorney, a couple of days' suspension, a week or two in detention, some mention about her Permanent Record, lots of strange looks and whispered comments from students and teachers, social isolation through June, and eventually, somewhere late in her senior year, a grudging acceptance back into the fold as her classmates focused on the phony nostalgia that was required near graduation.

If it *didn't* play out that way, if she didn't do all the stupid things the caller told her to do, didn't obey that mystery voice that knew her secret? She knew what that would be like too.

She paused at the bottom of the stairs, breathing in slow, then out slower, finding her focus, her game face, her thumbnail biting into the side of her finger, an old habit that explained the thin, curved scars.

That's when she saw her.

Locker open, books stacked on the floor, her back to the stairwell.

Just get it over with, Shelly thought, then moved without thinking, slipping into the hallway, letting the door close slow and soft behind her. It was too late to run, too late to get help, too late for both of them.

Shelly drew in one last deep breath, gritted her teeth, and smiled.

"*There* you are, Heather."

The girl jumped and spun around, her purse spilling open, the plastic case of her phone shattering as it hit the tile floor.

It didn't take long.

Less than a minute.

The girl standing still, eyes wide, too scared to move.

Like the last time.

Shelly trying to get it all out in one go, knowing she couldn't start it back up if she stopped, knowing that there was worse to come.

They were just words, she had told herself. No one gets hurt from words these days. She knew the truth but held on to the lie, the only way to get through it.

And then it was over, the girl's sobs fading in the distance, Shelly pushing the crash bar on the exit, stepping out into the blinding afternoon sun.

FOUR

THE HOUSE WAS EMPTY, BUT THEN, IT USUALLY WAS.

Shelly locked the door behind her, dropping her backpack on the floor by the kitchen table. There was a note from her father on the counter. She didn't have to read it, since she knew it would only be a variation of the same note he left every day. He'd start with an obligatory reminder about doing homework, then instructions on heating up whatever was in the fridge, the standard permission to order a pizza if that's what she wanted, a line about doing the dishes or the laundry or running the vacuum, and a final bit about not bothering to wait up for him, signing it "Jeff," or "J," or not signing it at all.

It was the same note he had left her every day since she had moved in.

Her father was at work by the time school let out, and got home an hour after she had gone to bed. The B shift paid more, and the overtime was too good to pass up. At least, that's what he told her.

In the bathroom, she washed off what was left of her makeup and brushed her teeth for the tenth time that day, the sour milk taste refusing to go away. She undressed and stepped into the shower, adjusting the temperature up as hot as she could take it. She stood there under the spray for twenty minutes, the hot water turning warm, then cool, then cold. Her teeth chattered between blue lips as she dried off. She put on a pair of sweats and wrapped her hair in a towel.

A week ago, she would have blasted some music — something scary, pounding, fast and loud — poured a glass of sweet tea, lit a few candles, and gotten her homework out of the way before crashing on the couch for a few sitcoms, then gone up to her room, where she would have read until she fell asleep. Now she sat curled up on the floor by the couch, backpack unopened, TV off, all the lights on, waiting for the phone to ring.

Her old friends — the few she had — had disappeared before she moved, and frankly, she couldn't blame them.

They knew.

Even if they had her new phone number — and no one from that life did — they wouldn't use it.

So no calls from them.

The friends she was *this close* to making — the ones who only saw her as the new girl in school, the ones who liked to sit with her in French class or hang out in the cafeteria or talk about music, the ones who made her laugh and forget — they would have texted, since that's how she got in touch with them. That, and nobody called anybody anymore.

So when the first call came almost a week ago, she had assumed it was a wrong number. Why else would her phone ring?

It had been hard to hear through the pops and hiss of static, and after she had heard her name, she had to concentrate to make out what the shrill, high-pitched voice had said.

She knew as she heard them what the words had meant. And what they meant for the new life she was starting.

Was the call really only five days ago? It felt like forever.

After an hour of sitting motionless on the floor, thinking, planning, she went back into the kitchen. Her head was pounding. The Tylenols she had dry-swallowed on the walk home had done nothing. Her stomach growled, and while the thought of food made her sick, she hoped eating something would help. She made a slice of dry toast, then a second, this one with butter and strawberry preserves, then she scrambled an egg and poured a glass of skim milk, adding in a squeeze of chocolate syrup. It wasn't a lot, but it was more than she'd eaten at one time in days.

Back on the floor, plate balanced on her knees, she tried to think about anything but school or Heather or the caller and the stupid tasks, and when she sensed her mind drifting back to her old life and *that night,* and the nights and days that had come after, she turned on the television, jacked the volume, and forced herself into a *Two and a Half Men* marathon.

The credits were rolling at the end of show number eight when her phone rang.

She let it ring a few times, then answered, knowing who'd be there.

"Three tasks down," the caller said. "One to go. Then the big finish next week."

Shelly stuck to her plan, not saying anything at first, letting the static-filled silence build. "How do I know you'll keep your end of it?"

"I guess you don't," the caller said, and even through all the audio effects Shelly could hear the laugh in the voice.

"So why should I bother?"

"Because if you don't, you know what I'll do."

There was another long pause, then Shelly said, "I'll do it one more time, but I can't do the last thing."

"That's the best part. And you don't have a choice."

"I don't have a video camera."

"Use your phone, stupid."

"It's an old phone. It doesn't have video."

"That's your problem."

"Even if it did, I can't hold a phone and do it at the same time."

"Then ask a friend to help."

"I don't *have* any friends. But you probably knew that already."

"All I know," the caller said, "is that if you don't do the video next Thursday, everyone finds out your secret."

Shelly took a deep breath, pushing down the rising panic. "I told you I'd do what you wanted, and I'm doing it, okay? But I don't know how I'm supposed to get the video. And even if I get it, I don't know how to do the rest. I'm not good with computers. If I could, if I had a decent phone and I knew how, believe me, I'd do it. But I can't, so you'll just have to come up with something else."

The static was gone and so was the caller.

Shelly hit last-call return and got the same recording as last time, telling her that the phone feature she wanted was not available with her cheap-ass plan. She clicked the phone shut and waited for the stomach cramps to start, but after ten minutes she still felt fine, and after another fifteen she noticed she was hungry again.

Hungry and pissed.

She'd come too far, endured too much.

And she wasn't going back.

Shelly nuked a bowl of ramen noodles and thought about Heather Herman. She was probably an okay person, friendly, fun to be around in her own mousy way. She liked *The Walking Dead,* so she couldn't be that bad. Maybe if things had been different, they could have been friends. A lot different, yeah, and maybe not *friends*, but not this. Heather was in the Drama Club, and Shelly always got along with the artsy types, mostly stoners, but still. The soccer thing she didn't get, and they definitely had different music tastes, but Heather was right about the double-chocolate fudge at Moonlight Creamery. Crack on a waffle cone.

It was the way she just *stood* there and took it, looking up at Shelly with those baby blue eyes and that trembling lower lip, the tears and the snot, letting some unknown transfer tenth-grader tear into her like that. It would be so much easier if Heather took a swing at her or kicked her or something. Especially since it was all bullshit anyway. Come on, a girl like Heather a slut? Yeah, right.

The microwave beeped, and Shelly ripped the rest of the lid off the plastic bowl. She stirred the steaming noodles with the chopsticks she had saved from the sushi place and mixed in a long splash of soy sauce. She knew she wouldn't finish it all, but it was what she wanted, and besides, there wasn't much these days that she wanted that she was likely to get.

Why just stand there? Why not *do* something? *Anything.* If this girl wasn't going to hit her, she could at least scream. That would get noticed. The more Shelly thought about it, the more she realized how easy Heather had it. She got to see the person who was talking shit about her, got to hear it, face to face, not whispered behind her back or finding it written on her locker. And she didn't have to wonder who it was who called her names from across the crowded lunchroom or who left her notes inside her backpack. Shelly could only guess what it would be like to be on the receiving end of what she was doing to Heather, but she knew whatever it was like, it had to be easier than the way the world had treated her when they found out what she had done.

She also knew it would only be a matter of time before Heather broke down and told A Concerned Adult like the posters said to do, and she'd be busted and that would be the end of it.

But the caller wouldn't care.

Something about the voice — the attitude behind the special effects — told Shelly that there would be no negotiating, no options, no mercy. No other way to keep everybody from finding out her secret.

So she'd stay with it, keep doing what the caller said.

Until she got busted, anyway.

And she'd listen to every whispered threat, waiting for the caller to make a mistake.

FIVE

ERIC OPENED THE STAIRWAY DOOR AND STARTED DOWN the hallway to the cafeteria, where he would share lunch with a stranger.

He was supposed to be in physics, but it was the only time the stranger — a freshman — was available. Eric hadn't skipped a class since he was in ninth grade, but nobody was going to stop him to check for a hall pass. And getting busted for missing class? That was the least of his worries.

He passed two girls on their way to the library, Red Bulled up, trying to be quiet, their racing whispered words blending into high-pitched static. They kept a death grip on their pink hall passes, clearly not wanting to find out what would happen if they were caught without them. What would happen would be nothing, just a couple nights' detention and a phone call home. But at that school, in that part of town, where every student went on to college and no teenagers ever got pregnant and every kid was above average, it could be trouble.

Not as much trouble as he was about to get in, but there was nothing he could do about that.

Anyway, it wasn't like he was about to totally ruin his life forever.

A year or two tops. But hardly forever.

It was all ninth-grade English classes this side of the building, and a late September heat wave kept the doors open. He recognized the teachers' voices, recognized the short stories the students were supposed to have read, the assignments they were supposed to turn in, the tests they were being prepped to pass. It was the same stuff they had said when he was sitting in there. He'd aced it all, and he didn't think he'd have any problems this year. But who knew what would happen after today.

Halfway there.

He could turn around, head back down the hall, or cut through the library, up the main stairs to the science department. Mr. Harkness wasn't the kind of teacher you could bullshit, so there'd be that detention and that phone call and blah, blah, blah, and if that was all there was to it, great, he'd take it. But he knew that if he turned around now, he'd never go through with it, and he had to go through with it. Besides, this was it, the last task and it'd be over.

He kept walking.

A kid came out of the boys' room, wiping his hands on the front of his jeans. He was a scrub on the JV team, and Eric had played against him in scrimmages, but that's about all he remembered.

"Hey, Eric," the kid said, smiling as he walked past.

"Hey," Eric said, no idea what the kid's name was.

Now, if it was some kid like that — smaller and younger, sure, but strong enough to take care of himself, tough enough to fight back — it wouldn't be so bad. It'd still be bad, no getting around that, but at least that way people might think it was some stupid jock thing that should've been left on the field.

But it wasn't some kid like that, and there was no way anybody would buy that story.

Eric made the turn at the end of the hall and walked into the cafeteria. There was that unmistakable smell, the sweaty air thick with pasta, steamed carrots, milk, grease, and plastic. Some days the smell was overwhelming, not enough to make you gag but enough to make you stick to the shrink-wrapped sandwiches. It was also first lunch, mostly ninth-graders, and that meant clouds of candy-sweet perfumes and musky body sprays that were more nauseating than anything the cooks could create. Another reason to get this over with.

There were a couple of tables of sophomores and juniors off in the far corner, their complex schedules requiring them to eat lunch two hours after they woke up. Eric wasn't in band and he didn't have a job and he did his community service on the weekends, so he had a normal eleventh-grade schedule with a normal, close-to-noon lunch. It was still too early in the year for the cafeteria monitors to know who belonged in which period, though, so no one stopped him when he walked in, and no one asked him why he wasn't in class. He would have lied, anyway.

Eric scanned the room, spotting Ian right where he'd said he would be, sitting alone as always, his backpack hiding the video camera. Ian gave a slow nod, and Eric nodded back. The guy was a freak—part hacker with a mercenary attitude, part scary loner with a juvie record and a reputation for packing a knife. When Eric had told him what he needed done, Ian didn't ask why, didn't ask any of the questions Eric knew his friends would have asked. He just stated a price, take it or leave it. Eric took it.

Eric picked up a tray from the stack, shook the water off by habit, and started down the line.

Pizza bagels, chili hots, two types of salad, two types of vegetables—the usuals. It didn't matter what was on the Today's Specials menu. He'd been told what to get.

The lunch lady smiled up at him. She was short and round and spent her days serving processed food to ungrateful teens and condescending adults. And still she smiled. "What would you like, hon?"

Eric stared into the fogged-up glass as if he was trying to make up his mind.

"Did you see we have pizza bagels? Those are popular. And there's a few turkey sandwiches left in —"

"Three mac and cheese, please."

There, he said it.

She laughed at him. "*Three?* You don't want *three*. That's too much, hon, even for you."

"I guess I'm really hungry," he said, not bothering to sound convincing.

"Why don't you start with one," she said, digging an ice cream scoop into the pan of neon-yellow macaroni. "If you want more, there's plenty here."

"No, I want all three at once. On the same plate."

She gave him a look.

"Please."

She shook her head, and the smile was gone. "You're just going to end up throwing it away," she said as she piled it on, slipping an extra paper plate underneath before she set it on the counter. She said something else, something about wasting money and proper nutrition and making sure this kid was charged for three entrees, but he had already moved on, punching his student ID number into the keypad by the register, then heading for an open table without stopping to get a plastic fork.

There were still thirty minutes left in the period, time to let the mac and cheese cool down a bit. He owed the kid at least that much. He used the time to look around the room, see who'd be coming to the rescue. It'd be a teacher or one of the aides. He didn't worry about the kid's friends — they weren't the type to do a thing, even if it happened to them. It made it easy. And that made it worse.

The first time, the kid had been alone, walking down a back hallway near the shop classes. A simple shoulder check into the lockers, books and papers everywhere. Eric had hoped that would be enough, but apparently it didn't count. Three days later he did it again, same move, close to the same spot, same results. Only this time Eric made sure the kid had a couple of friends with him, friends who backed off fast, waiting down the hall for it to be over. Now there was just this last thing to do and it would be over.

Well, the caller part, anyway.

He sat there looking around the room, his leg bouncing, the dirty-sock smell rising up from the tray in front of him. Out of the corner of his eye, he could see Ian tightening the strap on his backpack. Ian wouldn't get busted. He never did, not for anything. That's why he could charge so much. He'd slip out during the commotion, the teachers running past him to get to Eric.

The cheese started to harden. Eric stuck his finger in the middle of the yellow mound. It was warm but not hot. He rubbed the goo off on a napkin, took a deep breath, then stood up and headed across the cafeteria.

The kid was sitting with some other freshman. They were all alike — scrawny necks, big eyes, Old Navy tees, none of them needing to shave, uncoordinated, a bit goofy-looking, like baby birds. Just like he looked back then.

The instructions were to walk straight at the kid, let him see who was coming, see if that would make him freak or scream or, better yet, cry. But Eric wanted to get it over with, so he came in from the side, and he was standing over the kid before anyone realized what was happening.

Connor Stark: 127 Facebook friends, 0 in common. Likes Friendly Fires, Two Door Cinema Club, Foster the People, *Avenue Q, RoboCop, World War Z,* and Piranha Sushi Bar & Grill.

That was everything Eric knew about him.

So the kid looked up.

Looked right at him.

Eye to eye.

Just for an instant.

In that instant, Eric knew how it would all turn out.

And he did it anyway.

SIX

"Is there anything you want to add before we finish up here?"

Shelly kept her eyes on the brass-and-wood nameplate on the desk — SISTER TERESA KEYES, SSJ, PRINCIPAL — and kept her thumbnail pressed hard against her index finger. It hurt enough to keep her from saying something stupid.

"Shelly?"

"No, Sister."

Sister Teresa held her pose — head tilted forward, glasses balanced, one hand propping open a file folder, the other gripping a red pen — waiting for Shelly to look up. When Shelly didn't, she let the folder close, took off her glasses, and leaned back in her chair. She was the only nun at St. Anne's, but she didn't wear a habit. Other than the small gold cross that all but disappeared against her harvest-yellow sweater, she blended in with the other dowdy women at the school — she could have passed as somebody's mom. Shelly didn't know her well enough to have an opinion one way or the other, but she was sure Sister Teresa had made up her mind about her.

"Starting at a new school is always difficult," Sister Teresa said. "There are a thousand emotions going through your head, and at times it can all feel so overwhelming. But that does not excuse your behavior. Would you agree?"

"Yes, Sister."

"Now, you seem like a nice young lady —"

Face blank, Shelly laughed to herself.

"— and your records from your last school don't indicate anything to the contrary."

Check the other records, Shelly thought.

"I think this recent behavior is simply a reaction to the stress of moving and changing schools —"

If only it were that simple.

"— and frankly, I don't think it's the kind of thing you'd normally do."

You have no idea what I've done.

"Now, I could recommend that you be expelled, but I don't think that would be in anyone's best interest."

Ask Heather what she thinks about that.

"When you've completed the program I discussed — and your suspension is over — you'll be welcomed back."

Unless you learn the rest.

"But I think we both know that there's something bigger going on here."

Shelly looked up at the nun, careful not to give anything away.

"This . . . incident? It's a symptom of something else, something deeper, something that won't go away on its own. You need to figure out what's really behind all of this. And once you know what that is, you need to find a way to deal with it for good."

Shelly thought a moment, then nodded. "You're right, Sister. That's exactly what I have to do."

His phone buzzed and Duane's picture came up, flipping him off.

There was a chance Eric wasn't supposed to have his phone. His parents had mentioned something about taking it away when they were picking him up from the principal's office, but technically they never came out and asked for it. He was holding out, hoping their hard-line approach was only for show. Just to be on the safe side, he went into the garage before answering.

"That was stupid," Duane said, that smart-ass smirk in his voice.

Eric sighed. "Yeah, that's what they keep telling me."

"Nobody saw it. You should have waited until third lunch."

"I think a lot of people saw it."

"Freshmen and band geeks? They don't count. I mean, if you're going to do something epic like that, you could at least have the courtesy to do it when I can see it."

"Sorry. I'll check your schedule next time."

"Three things I like to see: the Yankees win, the Red Sox lose, and some funny-assed shit in the middle of my day. And that, my friend, would have been classic funny-assed shit."

"Trust me, it wasn't that funny."

"Coach is gonna be pissed," Duane said, turning the word into two, overinflected syllables. "You might get your ass kicked off the team there, pal."

"Yeah, maybe. We'll see."

"Hope it was worth it."

Eric didn't say anything.

"The kid step on your toe or something?"

"No, nothing like that," Eric said. "I guess I just felt like doing it."

"I can relate. I feel like that about every freshman. What's his name?"

"Connor Stark."

"No idea. Is he on JV?"

"I doubt it. I think he's a drama nerd."

"Even better," Duane said. "So, what's going to happen to you?"

"I find out tomorrow."

"I bet it's two days' suspension and a shitload of community service. Plus an extra two miles a day from coach and a couple hundred bleachers. That is, if he doesn't kick your ass off, right there. Your parents gonna come in to school to hear the verdict?"

"Oh yeah."

"They'll pile it on, just to show what good parents they are. My guess is you lose the car till Christmas or until they forget, whichever comes first."

"They won't forget," Eric said, then it got quiet for a second and he was tempted to ask Duane if he'd seen April that day, but he knew what he'd hear: Duane saying "Get over it" or "Move on" or his new one, "That ship has sailed." So he said nothing.

"Right. I'm gone. If by some miracle they let you out this weekend, a bunch of us are going to Frederico's. Play some FIFA, probably order pizza. Wings."

"Sounds boring."

"Agreed. But his sister Sophia will be there, and that's all I need to know."

Any other time, Eric would have laughed and told him she was out of his league, but he wasn't in the mood, and besides, it would no doubt end up with Duane saying something about April, and he didn't want to hear it.

"I'd wish you luck tomorrow, my friend," Duane said, the smirk back in his voice, "but I don't think it's gonna help."

Eric sighed again. As bad as the punishment would be, it would be nothing compared with what would happen if the caller decided to share his secret. "Yeah, one way or the other, I'm pretty much screwed."

"And not in a good way."

SEVEN

Ms. Owens POINTED THE REMOTE AT THE SCREEN, PAUS-ing the video when the words PAUSE HERE appeared, then read the folded paper in her hand. "Question one. What did you think of the video clip you just saw?"

It was 8:45 in the morning. Eric was sure that the people in the class — Ms. Owens, nineteen students, and a security guard — weren't thinking a thing. They all had that glazed-over, just-got-up-and-already-exhausted look that went with any first-period class, only this was Saturday, so it was worse.

His father had gotten him out of bed at six, using that rare voice that told Eric he'd better move it. His parents had let him drive himself, but it was more out of convenience for them than trust in him.

He'd arrived at the Jefferson County Community Center at seven, twenty minutes before the first staff member pulled in. There were a handful of cars in the parking lot, most with a kid in the passenger seat and a stern-faced parent behind the wheel. He recognized the look — part anger, part shame, big part disappointment.

It was the look he'd been getting since "the incident," his mother's new favorite phrase.

It was 8:20 before Ms. Owens started collecting paperwork and putting X's next to names on her list. The letter from the district said that mandatory check-in time for HABIT — Helping Accused Bullies by Inspiring Tolerance — was 7:30 sharp, and that under no circumstances would anyone be admitted late.

They were *all* late, and yet here they were, the tone of the day set before it started.

When she put the DVD in, there were only twelve students in the classroom, the others trickling in, taking open seats that were as far apart as possible. They didn't know each other, didn't want to know each other, didn't want to be there, and didn't care if it showed.

Some had a hard time playing it cool. One of the younger boys, maybe seventh grade, was too nervous to fake it, his head on a swivel as he scoped out the room. The girl with the Muslim headscarf was in her own world, scribbling tiny notes along the margins of the registration form they never collected. The Korean-looking kid kept his eyes on his hands, folded in front of him on his desk. The girl with the impossibly black hair, the one in the hoodie with the huge black patch that said KOMOR KOMMANDO — whatever that meant — looked pale enough to pass out, but it could have been some goth thing.

Everyone else, including him, went for bored indifference, the default setting of the guilty.

Ms. Owens unfolded the paper and tried again. "Was the film you saw realistic?" She waited, but no one wanted to be the first to speak. It was the opening session of a two-day program that would ruin the whole weekend. Say something cheesy now and that was it, you were the class suck-up, say something clever and you were the smart-ass, say something stupid and you were forever stupid.

"Did the film feel real to you?" She nodded at the screen, just in case they had forgotten what she was talking about. "Or did it seem a bit"— quick check of the paper —"exaggerated?"

Silence.

"I can start calling names," she threatened, lifting a clipboard from the table, but the odds were still good— almost one in twenty— so they waited. Ms. Owens forced a grin and looked at the roster. "Gregory Hodges?"

A black kid with a square jaw and a tribal tattoo band on his biceps rubbed his eyes. "It's too early for this shit. Call on somebody else, please."

"First, watch your language," Ms. Owens said, but the way she said it let them know that she didn't care what they did. "Second, everybody is going to participate, so you might as well get it over with."

"That's it? I answer and I can go?"

"If that's all it took, *I'd* answer the damn question," Ms. Owens said, chuckling at her attempt at a joke. "No, we're all here till two."

That brought the expected groans and mumbled swearing, but it wasn't news and there was no heart in it.

"So, Gregory—"

"Greg."

"Fine. Greg. What did you think of the film?"

A half shrug.

"That it?"

"Yeah, that's it."

"Did you think it was realistic?"

The other half.

Ms. Owens nodded. "We'll come back to you," she said, and looked at her clipboard. "Sara Zeidenberg?"

No answer.

"Okay, no Sara." She made a mark with her red pen. "Ryan Walker?"

"He's not coming."

She looked across the room at the girl with the short blond hair. "And you are?"

"Annalise Tutt. As in King."

"And you know Ryan how?"

"No, it's Ryan Walker. He goes to my school."

"And you know he's not coming because . . . ?"

"Because his father said this course is a waste of time and against his Eighth Amendment rights."

"Is that so?"

"He says it's cruel and unusual punishment," the girl said. "And that the school lacks legal jurisdiction."

"We'll see about that," Ms. Owens said, grinning like a shark, writing something hard and fast as she said it. "Rebecca Budinger?"

A girl with wavy brown hair stood up and started down the aisle. "I have to go to the bathroom."

"Are you Rebecca?"

"Yeah. I'll be back."

"Excuse me?"

The girl stopped at the door and looked over her shoulder. "Why, you gotta go too?"

The door closed behind the girl, and Ms. Owens stood there, waiting for the snickers and comments to trail off. Her fake smile was gone. She glanced over at the security guard, who was too busy with his phone to notice, then ran her finger down the list. "Eric Hamilton."

It figured.

Eric raised a hand, sort of.

"What do *you* think, Eric? Did the film seem realistic to *you*?"

"I guess," Eric said, and watched as her jaw tightened

and her one eyebrow quivered. That's when he knew Ms. Owens wasn't a real teacher. A few smart-mouthed teens first thing in the morning? Typical Monday in any high school. This woman? She didn't have the patience to be a teacher. Besides, a real teacher would have started off with some getting-to-know-you, wasting-time type of activity instead of just hitting PLAY and reading questions off a tenth-generation photocopy.

She wasn't a real teacher.

And that made her dangerous.

If she snapped now — and it looked like a real possibility — Eric knew she'd take it out on him, and that would only mean more problems, and he had enough problems to worry about. But he didn't want to be the suck-up either, so he played it flat and straight. "It seemed real to me. I don't know that school, but I guess it could be like that."

Ms. Owens narrowed her eyes. "What do you mean, it *could* be like that?"

"I don't know," Eric said, positive now that she was crazy. "I just guess it could be. It looked like a typical school."

"Did it look like *your* school?"

Oh, boy. "A little, I guess."

Behind him, a girl whispered something, and another held in a laugh, but the woman stayed hooked on him.

"So your school has bullies like the one in the video."

"Yeah, probably."

"Probably?" Her voice went up in that sarcastic, no-shit way. "I'd say your school has at least *one* bully, and his name would be Eric Hamilton."

"I'm not a bully. It's just that —"

"You wouldn't be here if *somebody* didn't think you were a bully. And that goes for all of you. You did something to end up here, and you've got to finish this program to be allowed back in the regular classes at your school."

Greg laughed at that. "Who said I wanted to go back?"

"I don't care what you do," Ms. Owens said. "You can leave right now if you want. Make my life a *whole* lot easier."

Greg shifted his legs and leaned forward, but that's as far as it got.

She looked at him. "If you're gonna go, go. Don't be wasting my time."

He waved her off, mumbling something that made the girl next to him giggle.

"Anybody else?" She scanned the room, making eye contact with those who looked up. "You don't wanna be here, go. I get paid whether you're here or not."

Eric looked at the clock. 8:49. Five hours and eleven minutes to go, with an hour off for lunch. And a half day tomorrow.

He'd never make it.

EIGHT

THE SECOND VIDEO CLIP WAS AS BAD AS THE FIRST.

The story picked up where the last part had ended, with Matthew, the skinny ninth-grader, getting jacked up by Chip, a senior who liked to snarl and put his finger in people's faces. Chip's surprisingly hot girlfriend seemed to get off on watching Chip punch people in the arm, moaning like a porn star when he put Matthew in a headlock.

It wasn't the over-the-top acting that made it so hard to watch — that was kind of funny — or the out-of-style clothes and haircuts or the twenty-five-year-olds playing high school students or the kid stars he recognized from '90s sitcoms playing teachers. It was the swearing, or lack of it, that made it so fake. It was hard to take the Chip character seriously when the worst thing he said was "butthead." And while Eric had never had a locker door slammed on his hand like poor little Matthew, he was sure that if he had, he would have said something worse than "Owie."

There was nothing in the video even remotely like Eric's situation. No dark-voiced midnight caller on Chip's phone, no threats to send out a damning photo to every-one Chip knew, no insane instructions about punking Matthew. Chip was just a regular, old-fashioned bully.

Eric knew he was different.

He didn't want to do any of it, but unlike Chip, he didn't have a choice. He did what had to be done, and that's all. He was paying for it now, which was fine by him since it was over, the caller's stupid instructions followed to the letter.

Most of them, anyway.

Enough to end the calls.

It had to be.

Ms. Owens waited until the screen said PAUSE HERE before mashing the button on the remote.

"Question one. What did you think of the video clip you just saw?"

After several painful minutes of grunted one-word answers, long silences, and laughable attempts at intimi-dating, authority-figure stares, Ms. Owens rewarded their apathy with a fifteen-minute break. Instantly, phones were out and the tapping started as everyone caught up on their texting.

Almost everyone.

It turned out his parents weren't showing off, and they now had his iPhone. But his mother still wanted him "reachable at any moment, anywhere," so she gave him the phone she had bought for her mother before her mother bought herself a Droid. It was the size of a paperback dictionary, with backlit numbers — each one as big as a dime — and a scratched-up display window that was hard to read. The ringtone was jet-engine loud, and there was no mute. He was able to transfer his iPhone number to this phone, and while he didn't expect anyone to call, even if they did, they wouldn't reach him, since he had accidentally left it on the kitchen table that morning, having waited until his mother went to refill her coffee before hiding it under the sports section of the newspaper.

The nervous kid asked if it was okay to get out of his seat and took Ms. Owens's mocking laugh as a yes. Several others followed him out into the hall, and after noticing that he was about to be the only one just sitting there, Eric went out too.

The hallway in the community center looked like a school hallway, but without the lockers and the trophy cases and the bulletin boards with reminders about SAT classes and the posters from expensive out-of-state colleges. Even without those extras, it still had that school-building feel — extra-wide stairwells, buffed tile floors, tan-gray paint, fluorescent lights, clocks that stuck sideways out of the wall, windows with wire in the glass.

Working in the building would be like going to school forever, and probably just as boring.

The girl with the headscarf was at the drinking fountain. Eric wondered what she had done. She couldn't weigh more than a hundred pounds, and it was hard to imagine her intimidating anyone with those big, sad eyes. The goth girl was buying a Diet Coke from the row of vending machines, and next to her, a black kid in a white shirt and tie loaded up on candy bars. Two janitors strolled by, talking over their parlay picks for the early Sunday games, both of them claiming that Buffalo was going to surprise some people. That made Annalise laugh. "Take the Raiders and the spread," she said, flashing a fake gang sign.

At least, Eric thought it was fake.

The nervous kid paced back and forth, turning to check the clock by the stairwell every thirty seconds. He'd put his hands in his pockets, then take them out, then put them back in, then let them hang by his side, then stuff them in again, the whole time chewing on his lower lip like it was a wad of gum. Whatever the kid had done, Eric decided, that was it, he was never going to do anything bad again for the rest of his life. He couldn't take it.

The tall kid with a fauxhawk — the one who had come into class halfway through the last video and left before it was over — punched open the men's-room door, swearing into his phone, telling whoever was on the other end about the dumb-shit losers he was forced to sit with in this bullshit class. He leered at the goth girl as he walked by, saying something about her ass, then bumped the nervous kid out of the way, popping a pack of cigarettes from his jacket pocket as he strutted down the hall. And it would have been impressive if he had caught it, but he missed, and it landed in front of him, so he had to do a little side-shuffle dance to avoid stepping on it. That brought on more swearing, and when he kicked the crash bar on the exit door, he lost his balance and stumbled forward, the door swinging shut and locking behind him.

Eric laughed along with the others in the hall, the goth girl smiling for the first time all morning. Even the nervous kid stopped chewing long enough to laugh. The fauxhawk? It was easy to see him as a bully. He had that piss-off look down cold, and he obviously liked to hit things. The cigarettes and the skull rings were part of the act.

The others?

Nothing about them said "bully."

They looked more like victims.

Okay, Annalise maybe, but she was the smart-ass type, a problem for teachers and vice principals, not other students.

The goth girl? The nervous kid? The Korean dude? The girl with the headscarf?

He wondered what they could possibly have done to get themselves sent here.

Then he wondered what they thought about him.

He didn't think he looked the part, but there he was, officially labeled a bully by the school district.

There they all were.

The security guard poked his head out and told them that break time was over. They started toward the class-room, then heard someone pounding on the exit door.

Pounding and swearing.

The stragglers in the hall looked at each other, waiting, listening, no one moving. Then Annalise grinned. "You heard the man," she said. "Break's over."

They all laughed again and, one by one, filed back in, a group now, whether they liked it or not.

The next session started with a ten-minute clip down-loaded from CNN about an antibullying program in Brockville, Ontario. Instead of kids who were bullied, the story focused on the ones doing the bullying, the reporter explaining that "getting these kids to admit that they have a problem is the first step on their long road to redemp-tion."

PAUSE HERE.

"Question one. What did you think of the video clip you just saw?"

Silence.

Ms. Owens snorted. "I *thought* so," she said, pulling a stack of blue booklets from a cardboard box on the floor. Eric knew what was coming next, and by the sighs from others in the class, they knew it too.

She passed around the stack, telling them to take one — and *only* one — and write their names, directory style, on the line next to where it said NAME on the cover.

"Directory style means last name first, first name last, then your middle initial," she said, although no one had asked.

Annalise looked up. "So it's middle initial last, first name second last, and last name third last?"

Ms. Owens shook her head. "Girl, just put your name on the book."

"I don't want to get it wrong."

"You will anyway," Ms. Owens said, and that got the guard laughing. She gave them five minutes to write their names, then took another minute to call up the writing assignment on the laptop and project it on the screen: *What actions did you take (or fail to take) that led others to identify you as a bully?*

"You can write in pencil or pen, I don't care," Ms. Owens said, "but you're gonna write."

The girl with the headscarf raised her hand. "If I fill

this book, can I get another?" Eric had expected an accent, something Middle Eastern maybe, or Indian, but there wasn't one he could hear.

"Girl, if it takes you more than one blue book to answer the question, then you are in a lot more trouble than I thought."

Somebody in the back said, "What's the minimum?"

"You start writing. I'll tell you when to stop. And don't tell me you 'did stuff,'" Ms. Owens said, putting air quotes around what they were all planning to say. "Be specific. Give examples. And remember, I have the reports on all of you already, so don't try to sugarcoat it."

The same voice asked, "What if I don't write anything?"

"Then you don't get credit for the assignment and I get to call your folks and tell them that you can't go back to school. Which is fine by me. My paycheck will be exactly the same either way. Now, the rest of you had better start writing."

Eric clicked his pen and opened the cover. An empty page with thin blue lines stared back at him. It was the same type of booklet they used for midterm essay tests, and he could hear every teacher he ever had telling him to rewrite the question at the top of the page because it would help him think of what to write. But he knew exactly what he had to write, the kind of things they were looking for him to say, saying it so it sounded the way they needed him to sound, whether he meant it or not, all those English classes about "knowing your audience" paying off.

He rewrote the question, then skipped two lines and started.

I was accused of —

Accused?

It would be great if that's all it was.

If he was simply *accused* of bullying, he wouldn't be here, his parents wouldn't be mad, he'd still be on the team, and maybe — *maybe* — April would talk to him again someday in this lifetime.

But he wasn't accused of anything.

He was guilty.

Eric crossed out the words, skipped another line, and started again.

I picked on —

Picked on? Cute.

You pick on your friends, teammates, girls who are one of the guys. It's what you do when you hang out, the thing that separates friends from strangers, the familiarity that made it funny and forgivable. But Connor wasn't a friend.

He crossed it out and skipped a line and told himself to just write the damn thing.

I bullied a kid.

He looked at the sentence.

Closer, but still not there yet.

Not "a" kid, a specific one.

A kid who never did anything, who didn't deserve any of it. A kid with a name.

I bullied Connor Stark.

Okay, how?

I called him names like —

That sounded stupid, and he crossed it out before he finished the thought.

I spoke insultingly to the young man at my school —

That sounded weird and somehow worse. He thought for a moment, then tried again.

I knowingly used insensitive and/or derogatory terms pertaining to sexual orientation to hurt another human being.

Better.

He was surprised he remembered it almost word for word from the *LGBT Diversity Education Facilitators' Handbook.*

That had been a great weekend.

April's older brother helped organize the summer training sessions during Gay Pride week at his college. He'd gotten April and Eric guest passes, even to the parties. They couldn't drink, but it was still a riot. Garrett wouldn't let them sleep in the same bed — *she's my kid sister, bro* — but they had time alone when Garrett was busy. They didn't push it, didn't go any further than they had gone before, but that was okay. It wasn't like it was his first or anything. Hers, yeah, but there was no rush. It'd happen when she was ready, and even if it didn't, that was okay too.

Because it was different with her.

Different and better.

Everything changed with April.

Especially him.

And then he'd thrown it all away.

Eric shook his head clear and read the line again: *I knowingly used insensitive and/or derogatory terms pertaining to sexual orientation to hurt another human being.*

It was accurate. It didn't say anything, but it was accurate.

Part of him wanted to write down everything he *had* said, word for word, put it out there in all caps, like it must have sounded when he said it. It didn't make any difference that he hadn't meant any of it. He'd said it and April knew it and that was it. And he knew as soon as he had said it that he would always be *that asshole, Eric.*

If he had just beat the kid up, it wouldn't have been as bad. Even the mac-and-cheese attack. But no, he had crossed the line, not with what he did but with what he had said. And not all of it, just three words.

Gay. Queer. Fag.

There were other words — nouns and verbs and adjectives, and words that used to be worse — but those three words were the ones that would hurt April the most.

And those were the words he had had to use.

The caller said so.

The other words? Just filler.

Eric took a deep breath and held it.

If I could go back, he thought, *would I do it again?*

Would I still say those things if I knew everything that would happen?

How much trouble it would get me in?

How bad I'd "disappoint" my parents?

Hurt April?

If I could go back, would I do it all again just to keep my so-called secret, keep that one stupid picture from getting out?

Eric thought about it for half a second.

Hell, yeah.

Down the hall, a door slammed, breaking his concentration. He stretched and looked around the room. A few of the others had their heads down on their desks, either done writing or done trying. The headscarf girl was still at it, the pages of the blue book filled, her tiny writing moving into the margins. The nervous kid was chewing on his pencil, deep in thought. Greg, the guy with the tribal tattoo, was already halfway through his blue booklet. Annalise was busy drawing pictures on the blank pages.

Eric stretched again, turning so he could see the goth girl.

Her book was closed, her pen down on the cover. She leaned on her elbows, her hands folded and resting against her forehead, eyes closed, lips silently moving, her face wet with tears.

NINE

THE ORGANIST HELD THE LAST NOTE OF "IMMACULATE Mary" until the stained-glass windows rattled, then he stopped cold, letting it echo across the wood ceiling like rolling thunder.

Not bad for a hymn.

Shelly listened as the organist shut the cover on the keyboard and locked the choir-loft door behind him, coming down the side stairs to the vestibule, joining the other old people as they shuffled out to the shuttle bus that would take them back to the nursing home.

She had the whole place to herself.

There probably was an altar boy or two in the back and some usher counting the collection-plate take, but out here where the pews were, it was empty and she was in no rush to leave.

There were two services at this church, 9:00 a.m. and noon. The noon service would be more crowded, since that was the mass with the priest who spoke English. The priest who did the early service was from someplace in Africa, and if Shelly didn't know the liturgy by heart, she wouldn't have had a clue what he was saying. As for the sermon, he could have been calling for a revolution for all she could make out. A lot of churches were doing that now, bringing in priests from Africa or China to make up for the shortages over here. Nonna Lucia didn't like it one bit. To her, every priest had to sound like Father DiPonzio, with a nice Italian accent, just like Jesus. It didn't matter to Shelly. She didn't come for the priest.

It had been different over at St. Mark's. The church was smaller, but more people came, and there were four services on Sunday and one on Saturday night, but why someone would spend any part of a Saturday night in church was beyond her. She used to like to go to the 10:45 service on Sunday mornings, since that was the one with the full choir and more songs, and Father Caudillo's homilies were usually funny and never depressing. The last time she had gone to confession it had been with Father C. He had listened quietly as she said what she had to say, and somehow she got most of it out okay, then he did his best, saying something about God's love and forgiving oneself and the difference between guilt and shame and what sin meant, and he told her a bunch of prayers she should say, as if prayers were going to make everything sunny and bright. She had said them anyway and — surprise, surprise — things started to change. Not a lot, no, and really slow, but it was something, or at least the hint of something.

Then the phone call.

Shelly closed her eyes and slouched down, letting her neck rest on the back of the pew.

Seriously, God, why you gotta be like that?

She knew there had to be *some* punishment. You don't commit a crime that big and expect to walk away. Maybe God was just picking up the slack for the judge. But it wasn't the voice of God that had her doing things she never thought she would do, things she hated doing but didn't have a choice about. Not a real choice, anyway.

She knew what would have happened if she hadn't done what the caller demanded, and she knew she couldn't go through that again. Better they think she was a bully than know the truth.

But what if she could have done things differently? Not with Heather Herman, but with the freak on the other end of the phone. What if she had the power to go back and start again?

Shelly smiled and imagined a better reality.

First, she needed to find out who was behind the calls. That had been her original plan. She'd thought it was going to be easy — download an app or something. They do it all the time on TV. What had come up on Google, though, was way, way over her head, so that plan fell through. But she was daydreaming now, and in that reality she'd get the number and she'd ring up the caller, playing it off movie-villain cool. "Hi, this is Shelly. Let's talk." Then there'd be that moment when whoever it was on the other end would realize they'd made a terrible mistake. It would be her mature tone and easy manner that would make the caller sweat, wondering what Shelly would do next. It didn't matter that Shelly had no idea what that sort of thing would sound like — that wasn't important to the fantasy. After that, she'd make it clear that if there were any more calls, any more threats, there'd be a shit storm of trouble. And not law trouble either. *Real* trouble — the kind you can't get out of on a technicality. The caller would have squirmed at that, would've been like, "I swear, I'll go away, you'll never hear from me again. I'll never tell anybody what you did, how you killed that —"

"You are displaying much happiness on your face," the priest said, stepping back when Shelly jumped, her stifled gasp sounding like a scream in the empty church.

"I am most very sorry, miss," he said. "I did not mean at all to frighten you."

"No, it's all right." Shelly put her hand over her racing heart. "I was just thinking about something, that's all."

"I, too, often sit here and think. May I?"

"It's your church," Shelly said, sliding down to give him room to sit.

"It is more your church than it can be mine, as I have only been blessed to be here for two months."

"That's about a month longer than me."

"So then we are both new members. I am Father Joseph Mwojt, but please call me Father Joe." He held out his hand and she shook it.

"Shelly," she said.

"I am from the city of Nimule, at the very southern tip of South Sudan. And yourself?"

Shelly smiled back. "I used to go to St. Mark's church in Lockport. Ever hear of it?"

"There was a St. Mark's in Juba, the capital of South Sudan, but I assume that is not the one you mean." He laughed, and Shelly thought that even that had an indecipherable accent.

"I enjoyed your sermon today."

"Impossible. I myself could not understand what I was saying half the time." His smile was blinding white against his skin.

"Okay, so I didn't follow it all, but what I heard sounded good."

"Do you mean the beginning part when I said 'Good morning,' or the end part when I said 'God bless this day'?"

"Both. The stuff in the middle . . ." She shrugged, and that made him smile more.

"It was from the Gospel according to John, the story of Jesus and the woman who was to be stoned to death for her crimes. Do you know this story?"

It figures, she said to herself, and sighed. "Yeah, that's the old 'He who's without sin cast the first stone' one."

"Yes, you are one hundred percent correct. This is a very good Bible story, and it is also a humorous paradox, as none of us are without sin and therefore cannot condemn the sinner."

"Well, that's Jesus for you," Shelly said, trying to ignore the memories the story had sparked.

"Even those who think that their sins are secret must know that nothing is secret from God."

"Great, thanks for the reminder." She picked her hoodie up off the pew and stood. "Good luck on your sermon next week."

"Thank you, Miss Shelly," Father Joe said, stepping into the aisle. "God willing, I will speak on Proverbs nineteen-five. Do you know this as well?"

"Not off the top of my head."

"I am sure that you will recall it. It is all about the mortal sin of bearing false witness."

Shelly shook her head as she looked up at the stained-glass window high above the altar. "Seriously, God?"

"Excuse me, please?" Father Joe said.

She sighed again, and this time it trailed off into a hollow laugh. "I said, see you later."

TEN

ERIC RUBBED THE SLEEP FROM HIS EYES, TAPPED OPEN
the app, and checked his text messages.

His parents had his phone — probably would for weeks
— and while it was a pain in the ass, it wasn't the end of
the world. A couple of clicks and a password and every text
that was sent to his phone now appeared in a box on the
screen of his iPad. Texting back was harder, but only because he wasn't used to the wide keyboard.

Nothing new had come in since midnight, when Duane
had texted updates from Frederico's house, claiming that
he and Sophia were busy getting busy. That's how Duane
would have said it too — *busy getting busy*. And that's why
Eric knew Sophia would have laughed and walked away.

Emma had sent a text around eight, a long string of
question marks followed by an angry-face icon. He didn't
know if she was mad at him for what he did to Connor,
or at the principal for piling on the punishment. Probably
him, but Eric liked the idea that somehow she was on his
side.

There were no texts from April.

April.

It used to be so easy. In ninth grade there was Rachel; then, the night that ended, he met Simone, and that was great for a while, but then Simone heard about him and Juliana at Nick's party and dumped him, so he hooked up with Heluna, the exchange student from Finland. Then she was gone and it was on and off with Simone again, then Chloe, then back one more time with Simone.

And then there was April.

Just hanging out at first, just friends, both sure it was nothing more, talking all the time, movies, pizzas, late-night texts, imagine-us-dating jokes, the jokes becoming questions, the questions answered, then real dates and real talks and real time together, wonderfully different, so true it hurt, both of them sure it could never get better.

And then it didn't.

Hang-ups and voice mails and unreturned texts, his hoodie she'd loved to wear returned, balled up in his locker, the necklace handed back by a girlfriend, her Facebook status skipping *It's complicated*, going right to *Single*.

Eight weeks later, and it was still a blur.

All he had now were the memories.

The best ones of his life.

That and the chance that, who knows, maybe, somehow, someday, they'd get back together and it would be as good again.

Just a chance.

Okay, there still was the whole bullying thing, so un-April it'd be hard for her to forget, but there was a chance it could happen.

And that was all he needed.

The number nineteen bus swung through the parking lot and pulled up in front of the main entrance of the Department of Motor Vehicles. It made no sense, since the DMV was closed on Sundays, but the bus schedule said that the number nineteen would be there at 11:50, and it was, right on time. Nobody got on the bus and nobody got off, and at 11:51 the door closed with a hiss, the driver retracing his route through the empty parking lot, turning left onto Ridgeway Boulevard.

At 12:32 it would pull up in front of the Jefferson County Community Center, where Shelly would get off, twenty-eight minutes early for the second half of the program.

HABIT.

Helping Accused Bullies by Inspiring Tolerance.

Shelly wondered if they'd started with a title, rearranging the words until the initials spelled something catchy, or if they'd picked a word they liked and forced the title into it. She used the first ten minutes of the ride to come up with better names and acronyms, stopping when she knew she couldn't top Futilely Underfunded Course for Kids Unfit for Polite Society.

She had the bus to herself. There had been an old guy sitting in the seat right behind the driver when she got on at the stop near the church, but he got off two stops later, and no one else had gotten on so far. There was another bus — the number twenty-one — that would have been more direct, but she was going to get there early enough as it was, and besides, she liked buses, with their big windows she could lean against and watch the world go by. At least this little part of it.

Unfortunately, the longer ride gave her time to think. As if she wasn't doing enough of that anyway.

Shelly tried to remember what it was like to think about other things. There was a time — a thousand years ago — when she had an opinion on *American Idol* and dubstep and *World of Warcraft* and Taco Bell, getting into endless *The Walking Dead* vs. *American Horror Story* debates, reposting cat videos, re-tweeting one-liners. She wondered how she had been able to let go and let her mind wander in and out of dozens of random thoughts for hours on end. Maybe there was a trick to it that she'd forgotten, a way to escape the black hole that sucked her into the same endless loop of the same endless thoughts every time. If only she could remember how to do it, how to turn off her brain, she could go back to thinking about anything, even stupid stuff. Especially stupid stuff.

The bus stopped for a red light near a Starbucks, and for a moment Shelly relaxed and thought about coffee. Her brain gave her a minute or two alone with that before starting the downward spiral, switching slowly to donuts, moving on to chocolate donuts, then just chocolate, then fancy pieces of chocolate, then chocolate in a heart-shaped box, and then, inevitably, unavoidably, she thought about Valentine's Day.

This time the black hole was filled with voices.

The 911 operator pleading with her to calm down.

The EMT saying he wasn't getting any vital signs.

The police officer looking down at her, telling her she had better call her parents.

And playing under it all, like a movie soundtrack, the long, horrible scream, then the longer, more horrible silence.

The bus jerked forward, and her brain let her go.

Shelly breathed in deep and slow through her nose, holding her breath till her lungs burned, letting it out in little bursts the way Father Caudillo had shown her. He'd also shown her how breathing into a paper lunch bag would take the knot out of her stomach and keep her from panicking, but Shelly thought it made her look like she was huffing paint, so she stuck with the other technique, even though it didn't always work.

"Once you get your breathing back to normal," Father Caudillo had told her, "take control of your thoughts. Don't let your thoughts control you. You can't change the past, so don't waste time dwelling on it. Think about today, the things you have to do right now. Every journey begins with a single step in the right direction."

Head clearing, she thought about the next steps she had to take.

First, she had to finish the program. The whole thing was too nice to everybody, even the assholes. While most of the video screen time went to the victims — the old "building empathy" approach — they also showed life from the bullies' point of view, and what do you know, all the bullies, even Chip, turned out to be sensitive souls, fighting their own inner demons and lashing out at others as a coping mechanism. They didn't use those exact words, but Shelly could imagine that's what the script had called for. The problem wasn't that they were simply demented or cruel or violent — the problem was the issues that made them act that way.

Okay, that sort of explained *her* situation, but Shelly didn't think it held for the rest of them. Maybe that little boy. And the Muslim girl who wrote all those notes to herself. And maybe that cute guy, Greg. But the jerk with the stupid haircut who got locked out, or that jock who kept looking at her, or that scary girl with the neck tattoo, or the rest of them? They didn't need issues.

So, anyway, finish the program.

Then she had to write up a reaction paper for school, a ten-page essay that was supposed to show how much she had learned from the weekend session and how sorry she was for the things she had done to Heather, who she wasn't allowed to name in the paper or to ever speak to again. The paper would be easy. She could write ten pages in her sleep, especially when she didn't have to back any of it up with facts. As long as she kept her real emotions out and kept away from the truth, she'd be all right. As for inner demons, she had plenty, but she'd probably go with a combination new-girl-in-school/devastated-by-parents'-breakup. They weren't *her* inner demons, but she knew it would be the kind of thing that would click with the counselors.

Next she'd have to catch up on her schoolwork.

The suspension would keep her home all week, so her teachers were supposed to send her the work she had to do, and her father was supposed to pick it up in the main office, but she knew how that would play out. Between her father not remembering to swing by the school and her teachers sending cryptic assignments or forgetting to send anything at all, she'd be behind in every class when they let her back a week from Monday.

The math she could do on her own, and she could keep up with the reading for history. English was something different every day, but her teacher said that the reaction paper would go toward her first-quarter grade. They were going to be doing pottery in art class, and that was with Ms. Augustyn, so there'd be no making that up. In science they were dissecting mice. Missing that unit would be a good thing. French was just starting to make sense — a week out of class would leave her *dans la merde*.

As for the discussions in religion class, Shelly was pretty sure that she was the discussion.

So much for academics.

Her school required three hours of volunteer work each week. She had until the first week of October to sign up somewhere, and she was running out of time. When they first told her about the policy, Shelly had been tempted to point out the logical fallacy of required volunteerism, but she didn't think the people in the main office would share her appreciation of irony. Before the move, she had volunteered at a shelter that cared for rescued pit bulls, not because the school required it but because she wanted to. She was too young then to work with the dogs, so she had cleaned cages and filled food bins. It wasn't glamorous, but it still felt good, and the dogs seemed to enjoy her company. The first Saturday in February was the last time she had been there. She never went back. Better to walk away than to be told you weren't wanted.

She made a mental note to Google the address of the local animal shelter.

And, oh yeah, her mother's birthday was Tuesday.

She could buy a card on the way home, mail it first thing Monday morning. It'd get there on time. But why bother? She would never open it, Shelly was sure of that. Her mother didn't want to hear from her. Why would she? So that she could be reminded of what happened? Like she'd ever forget. She'd be better off pretending she didn't have a daughter. And as for the letters her mother had sent her? Straight to the trash. The phone messages? Deleted as soon as they came in. Shelly could guess what they said, the words her mother would use to describe her, the same words she had heard whispered in the corridors of her last school. And worse.

So no stupid card.

But there was one more thing she had to get done that week.

At least, that's what the caller had said.

Well, there was no way it was going to happen, so . . .

For one, she was suspended. If she went back to school early — for *any* reason — she'd get kicked out. Sister Teresa had made that clear. And it was no secret that she had to stay a hundred feet from Heather. If she so much as walked into the room where Heather was sitting, every teacher in the building would be on her.

Then there was the caller's ridiculous requirement that she video the whole thing and put it up on YouTube, which was impossible because her phone didn't have video. Besides, if someone else filmed it for her — nobody would, but saying they did — the cafeteria at the school didn't even serve macaroni and cheese. The closest they came was chili, and that was on Tuesdays. And this, for *some* reason, had to be on Thursday.

She didn't see any way to make it happen. Not by Thursday.

And this time next weekend, they'd know. Miranda Eduardo, the hyperexcited senior behind every fundraising event at St. Anne's. Deborah Knight and LJ Martin, the library geeks. Julie Redfern, future nun. They were the closest she had to friends since she'd arrived, and they liked her for who they thought she was.

But that would all change once they learned her secret.

The St. Valentine's Day Massacre, all over again, thanks to a voice on the phone.

Shelly spent the rest of the ride trying to think of some way out of it, but when the bus pulled up in front of the Jefferson County Community Center at exactly 12:32, she still had nothing.

ELEVEN

"**Question one. What did you think of the video** clip you just saw?"

There were only eight of them in the class.

Impossible to hide.

Ms. Owens had arranged the desks in a circle and made them tape sheets of paper with their names in block letters to the fronts of their desks. Eric had liked it better when they sat in rows. It was easier to ignore people, especially when you didn't know who they were. Now when one of them spoke, everybody looked.

Ms. Owens sighed. "Give me a break here, people. This is our last video clip, and then we're done. But I gotta have some participation before I let you go."

Annalise and the scared kid — whose name was Cody — raised their hands.

"I thought it was good," Annalise said. "I liked how it worked out like that in the end."

Ms. Owens nodded slowly. "You too, son? Okay. How about the rest of you?"

They all mumbled agreement.

"Think it was realistic?"

"Sure," Greg said. "Chip apologized and Matt said it was cool and they moved on. Done."

"I think Chip's girlfriend has a real attitude problem," the girl apparently named Docelyn said. "I don't know what he saw in her, anyway."

Eric and Greg exchanged knowing glances that made Cody giggle and Annalise and the goth girl roll their eyes.

Ms. Owens made them wait, then said, "What did you think of what Chip said to the counselor?"

The girl with the headscarf, Fatima, looked up from her scribbling and raised her hand. "I think it showed that he understood how Matt was feeling and how his actions were hurting other people. I think that that was his life-changing, empathetic, breakthrough moment," she said, checking her notes and lifting a line from the film.

"I see," Ms. Owens said, still nodding. "Any other thoughts?"

They all said no, that pretty much covered it, Fatima had said what they were thinking, each of them sneaking a glance up to the clock.

"Well," Ms. Owens said, really smiling for the first time. "Either you're all a bunch of liars, or you're dumb as posts. Which is it?"

A girl named Sandra sat up. "I don't like being called a liar."

"And I don't like being lied to. And for the record, you could have picked being called dumb." She rolled the TV cart out of the way and pulled up a chair. "Honestly, do any of you really think it's going to be that easy for you to go back to your school? That all it's going to take is one five-minute talk with a school counselor and everything is going to be fine? That the kids you bullied are going to forgive you? Ever? Their parents can still press charges — you know that, don't you?"

"I thought that this program —"

"*This?* Girl, please. This is a waste of your time, my time, Rick's time" — she nodded to the security guard — "taxpayer dollars, and the gas it took to drive you here."

Greg shook his head. "Then why are we here?"

"Because you *have* to be here. Your principals identified you as bullies, and in this county that means you have to attend this workshop and watch these videos — which *somebody* bought two years ago, sight unseen, and now we're stuck with them. And you were stuck watching them."

"If the program's no good, then why don't they do something better?"

"You don't deserve anything better, that's why. At least from their point of view. Remember, *you* are the problem," Ms. Owens said, making eye contact with each of them as she said it. "*You* are the bullies. *You* are the ones that ruin a school's reputation and lead to bad rankings on statewide lists. All this program does is remind you of who is really in charge. And it ain't you."

"Great," Annalise said, laughing. "So when I go back to school next Monday —"

"You're *still* the problem. And nothing's going to suddenly change, either. Your parents still won't trust you, your teachers will still assume you're a disciplinary issue, the good kids will still talk behind your back, the truly bad kids will laugh in your face. And the kids you picked on? Don't go trying to apologize to them. They don't want to hear it. In fact, they don't want you anywhere near them. And it's not just you, Annalise. That goes for all of you. Times are different. In my day, you'd get a night's detention maybe, and that'd be it. A week later, it was like it never happened, everybody movin' on. Now? It's going to stick to you like white on rice."

Eric tried not to smile. Yeah, there'd be some comments, but it wasn't like he knifed the kid or anything. Already his parents were softening up and his teachers were so worried about the next round of test scores that they'd welcome his curve-shifting average back to class. A quick glance at the others told him that they weren't buying it either. Well, except for Cody.

"Now, there's still hope for you," Ms. Owens said, building up for her big finish. "That's because you're still here. Aren't you curious what happened to the others? We started off with twenty, but you're the only ones left. Eight of you. That's all."

Cody raised his hand. "They didn't want to come here on a Sunday?"

"No one does. But that's not why they aren't here. Remember that essay you had to do yesterday? What you wrote told me whether or not you passed this course. That's it. Somebody writes about how *they* were the victim, that the school was just out to get them or that what they did wasn't so bad? I call my supervisor, tell her the kid was disruptive, she calls their parents, and that kid finds himself in a *different* program that's not nearly as much fun. You're here because you admitted the truth and took responsibility for what you did. And I think that's a good first step."

Greg smiled. "How do you know it wasn't just bullshit?"

"I don't. But I like to give people the benefit of the doubt. If you'd prefer, I can go back and reread what you wrote —"

"No, it's cool. I'm good."

"We'll see." She handed Fatima a stack of papers. "Now, these are what we send to your school to prove that you completed the program. Fill in your name—directory style, Miss Annalise—and the other information on all five sheets, then pass them back to me to sign off on and we'll be done here."

It took a few minutes for everyone to find or borrow a pen, then it got quiet as they filled in the form. Off to the side of the room, Ms. Owens had the security guard laughing as she recounted what some of the missing students had written in their essays. It was impossible not to listen in.

"... claimed it was his twin brother who, by the way, is two years older ..."

"... said she didn't remember it, so it didn't count anymore ..."

"... part of a community-service project to raise awareness about bullying ..."

"... said a strange voice had called her at night—"

Eric's head snapped up. Eyes wide, he held his breath, waiting for more, but Ms. Owens had moved on to other unbelievable excuses.

That's when he noticed the goth girl staring at him.

He looked across the circle and stared right back.

She didn't look away.

Her eyes stayed locked on his, her expression hardening with each heartbeat.

He blinked, then rubbed his chin and returned to the blank spaces on the form.

When he glanced up a minute later, she was still watching him.

She nodded once — slowly — then flipped a page and went back to writing.

TWELVE

ERIC WAS PUSHING OPEN THE DOOR AT THE END OF THE hall when he felt a tug on his sleeve. He looked down at the hand gripping his sweatshirt. Silver rings with skulls and stars and sharp points, stubby black fingernails. Then up the black sleeve of her hoodie, past the black-on-black band patches to that mass of purple-black hair. Then at her dark eyes, made darker by her makeup and the way she was glaring at him.

"I *said* hello."

It wasn't a friendly look. He was ready to say hello, and then goodbye and walk off, when she said, "We need to talk."

"I'm pretty much talked out today," Eric said, easing his sweatshirt from her grip and starting down the stairs. But she stayed with him.

"*Listen* to me. We know someone in common," she said.

He turned and looked at her again and got the same icy stare. He shook his head. "I seriously doubt it."

"Well, you're wrong. We do. And that's why we need to talk. *Right now.*" She grabbed for his sleeve, he stopped short, and she bumped into him. He matched her expression.

"Look, I don't know you —"

"I'm Shelly Meyer, you're Eric Hamilton. We've been sitting in the same room together for two days."

"Great. And now it's over. Goodbye."

He jumped the last steps and headed toward the parking lot. She watched from the top of the stairs, waiting until he had crossed the bus lane, then she drew in a deep breath and cupped her hands around her mouth to target her shout.

"It's about your secret."

Eric stopped midstride, stumbling forward, then spun around, his body reacting to the words his mind was still processing.

"The caller knows," Shelly said, still way too loud, Eric sprinting back at her, "and if we don't do something, so will —"

He leaped up the stairs, teeth clenched. "What the hell are you doing?"

She dropped her hands and lowered her voice. "Getting your attention."

He looked around — no one watching them — then stepped in close. "All right, let's talk."

She gave a flat smile. "I thought you were all talked

out." He narrowed his eyes at that, so she continued. "I saw your reaction back in the room. Somebody called you, said they knew your secret and made you punk that kid."

"How'd you—"

"Duh. Obviously I'm getting the same calls. That's why I'm here too." She watched his expression, waiting for the doubt to disappear. "The voice is altered, right? And the caller tells you *exactly* what to do and when to do it?"

He raised an eyebrow.

Shelly leaned forward. "Including the mac and cheese."

"How do you know that?"

"*You are not listening,*" she said, her voice rising as she tapped the side of his head. "I got the same calls."

He ignored the tapping and looked into her eyes. "You got a call telling you to—"

"To pick on a *specific* girl on *specific* days, and that I was supposed to dump a plate of macaroni and cheese on her head at noon next Thursday and post it on YouTube, yes."

"So you have some sort of secret."

"We all do. But the caller knows mine. And apparently yours, too."

Eric looked away. "I don't know what you're talking about."

Shelly laughed. "A little late for that, don't you think? Listen, I don't want to know your secret, and I'm certainly not going to tell you mine. But if we work together, we can figure out who's behind this and stop it before it gets worse."

"Why don't you figure it out yourself?"

"I could," she said, the sarcasm close to the surface. "But I'm running out of time. And so are you. That's why you have to help."

He looked down at his sneakers, scuffing them against the concrete step, thinking, then looked back up at her dark, determined eyes.

"No, thanks," he said, and started back toward the parking lot.

Shelly stood motionless, not breathing, as she watched him cut around an idling Escape, watched him wave as Greg rode by in a parent-driven SUV, watched him pull his car keys out of his jeans pocket and head toward a faded blue Toyota. Then she ran after him.

"What do you mean, *no*?"

"You don't have to shout," Eric said, pointing the key chain and unlocking the car door. "I'm right here."

"You *have* to help."

"I don't have to do anything," he said. "Besides, it's over."

"Over?" Shelly made a noise that could have been a laugh. "It hasn't even *started* yet."

"Stop shouting," he said. Then he sighed and ran a hand over his face. "Look. I know you're mad. I'm mad too. We got played, it sucks, life goes on."

She took a step closer and lowered her voice. "Really?"

"We can't do anything about it now anyway."

"Yes. We. Can."

Eric pulled the car door open. "First of all, we don't even know who this guy is."

"First of all, it's a girl."

Eric stopped and looked at her.

"The voice is altered, right?"

"Yeah," he said. "But it's real deep, like he thinks he's Darth Vader or something."

"When she calls you. When she calls me, it's high pitched, like she's sucked helium."

"How does that prove it's a girl?"

"If it was a guy, he'd use a deep voice on both of us."

"And you know this because . . . ?"

"Because a guy doesn't think like a girl."

Eric smiled at that. "But a girl can think like a guy?"

"In this case, yes," Shelly said. "Pretend you got the same call, but this time it was from a girl. You wouldn't take her seriously."

Eric shrugged.

"For a guy, it's got to be a deep male voice. But you try

that with a girl, threatening her with a voice like that? No way. She's going to be too scared to move or she's going to call the cops. That's why it's a girl. She knows that she has to make it scary, but not too scary. A deep voice for you, a high-pitched one for me."

He let the door swing shut, then leaned against it, arms folded across his chest. "All right, fine, maybe it's a girl. We still don't know who it is."

"*But we can figure it out. It's gotta be somebody we both know or who knows both of us. All we have to do is figure out what we have in common and take it from there."

"Keep it down," Eric said. "As for your plan, that could take forever."

"Impossible. I don't know that many people."

"We wouldn't even know where to start."

"*Yes, we would,*" she said, her voice rising again, her hands chopping the air. "We'd start with the obvious stuff. School, sports, church—"

"I don't go to church."

"Great. That's one less area we have to check." She paused to catch her breath. "We can *so* do this."

Eric looked into her brown eyes, nothing like the sky blue he saw in April's. He started to say something, paused, chuckled to himself, and then said, "I don't want to know who it is."

"*What?*"

"I said I don't want to know." He kicked at the yellow line of the parking space. "It's no big deal."

Her eyes went wide, her mouth dropping open. At first she couldn't get the words out of her head, then they wouldn't stop.

"You . . . I . . . but . . . she . . . she's *blackmailing* you, you *idiot*. She's gonna *destroy* you. How can you say you don't want to know? You *have* to know, you have to *stop* her — *we* have to stop her. No big deal? *No big deal?* My god, she . . . she's gonna *tell* people. She's . . . she's *evil*. Don't you see it? You can't just let her do that to us."

Eric watched as she jabbed her fingers through her hair, grabbing a fistful in each hand, holding it as she squeezed her eyes shut and breathed through her nose in big, gulping breaths. He was easing the car door open when she looked back up at him, her eyes narrowed and cold.

"You did it, didn't you?"

He looked away. "Did what?"

"Oh my god. You did," she said, laughing now. "I can't believe it. It's crazy. You went through with it."

"Calm down. You're the one who's crazy," he said. "I don't know what the hell you're talking about."

"No, please," Shelly said, stepping forward, her hand on his forearm, her voice soft, pleading. "Just tell me. I need to know."

He stopped, and she waited until he looked back down at her.

"You did everything she told you to do, didn't you?"

"No," he said. "Not everything."

"Like . . . ?"

"I skipped a couple of the days, the harassing-in-school stuff. I figured he'd — *she'd* — never know."

"The macaroni and cheese?"

He looked away, smiling an embarrassed smile.

"Wow," she whispered, her expression changing, mirroring his. "How did you . . . ?"

Eric held out his arm, palm up, then flipped his hand over.

"Yuck."

"The guy who videotaped it for me put it up on YouTube. It had close to four hundred hits before my little meeting with the admin. They assumed I was behind it and told me to take it down. I figured it was up long enough, so I had him pull it."

"A friend of yours?"

"More of an acquaintance."

They stood quiet for a minute, and when Eric sorted through his car keys and turned, Shelly said, "I didn't do it."

"*Any* of it?"

"Of course I did some of it. That's why I'm here. But

'concerned adults' intervened before I got to the . . . what-ever," she said, repeating his plate-flip gesture.

"Still gonna do it?"

Shelly grunted. "I can't."

"Sure you can," Eric said. "I didn't think I could either, but when it came down to it, I guess I figured I'd get in less trouble dumping mac and cheese on some kid than I would if, you know . . ."

"I agree."

"Then you gotta do what you gotta do."

"Believe me, I would," Shelly said. "But I can't get near her, I don't have a video camera, I'm not good with techni-cal stuff, and all we have is stupid chili."

The chili thing made no sense, but Eric knew where she was going. "You need my help to keep your secret safe."

"Exactly."

He shook his head. "No way. I'm in enough trouble. I do something like that again —"

"Not *that* kind of help. I wanna find out who's behind all of this and make her stop. I don't have time to do it alone. With two people we can cross-reference names, compare notes, look at things we have in common. Like I said, we can do this."

"And like I said, I don't want to know."

"You really think she's going to forget all about your

precious secret, that she's not going to hold it over you? Forever?"

Eric shrugged. "I did what she said to do. So, yeah, I think she'll keep her side of the deal."

"Then you're an idiot."

"Fine. I'm outta here."

Eric got in his car and started it up, buckling his safety belt and adjusting the volume down on the radio.

Shelly didn't move.

He could back out without hitting her, but it'd be close. Instead, he rolled down his window. "Look, I'm sorry. I'm not trying to be a dick about this —"

"You're doing a good job of it."

"— but I've got enough problems as it is. If I think of anything, I'll let you know."

"How?"

He went for his iPhone, remembering just in time the brick-size replacement his mother had made sure she handed to him before he left the house. He reached behind the passenger seat and pulled out his backpack, tore a page out of his science notebook, and passed her a pen. She used the hood of the car as a desk, writing her name in neat, Catholic-school cursive, and under it, her cell and home numbers. She handed him the paper, then asked for his number, and after a second's pause, he told her. She punched the numbers into her phone with one hand and held out his pen with the other.

"She's not going to let you go, you know."

"We'll see," he said, shifting into reverse and backing away from her.

THIRTEEN

THE SECOND QUARTER HAD JUST STARTED WHEN ERIC sat down. His father had the chips and salsa set out already, and his mother was cutting up the Italian subs she had picked up at the deli department of the grocery store. The Cowboys were playing the Steelers, and even though it was still September, the announcers kept talking about playoff implications.

The lectures and long silences had eased up, and it was back close to normal, at least when there was a game on. Eric grabbed a handful of blue corn chips from the bowl. "Did I miss anything?"

"A pair of field goals, a fumble, and that stupid dancing-robot commercial." His father sipped an Odenbach stout, a dark beer that looked black and tasted like tar. And he drank it warm, which made it even more disgusting. Eric preferred Corona, but since he was underage and only drank at parties at friends' houses when their parents were out of town, he stuck to Coke.

"Any other games on?"

"Yeah, but I've got Pittsburgh's defense and a Dallas

tight end on my fantasy team. I want to see how they look. We'll switch over at the half."

The Cowboys had the ball, and they were taking their time moving it down the field, Eric and his father pointing out fouls that weren't called and open receivers who should have been covered. A run up the middle ended with a pileup at the forty, which led to an injury time-out. His father waited until the commercials started.

"How was your session?"

"It was okay," Eric said, and normally that would have been it, a few grunted answers and I-don't-know shrugs. But he knew he wouldn't get away with that until the whole thing was far enough behind him that they stopped looking for a reason to punish him some more. Till then, they got specific details, complete sentences, plenty of eye contact, and no attitude. "We watched the rest of the film and talked about stuff like our behavior and what we need to do to get our lives back on track. There were only eight of us today, so it was easier to get everybody involved."

"Where were the rest of them?"

"They got kicked out," Eric said, exaggerating the little he knew for effect. "Ms. Owens said that they didn't accept responsibility for what they did, and that that was one of the things you have to do to complete the program."

His father looked at him. "What about you?"

"I'm done. Today was the last day."

"Not that," his father said. "Do you accept responsibility for what you did?"

"That's what the essay was about. It was, like, ten pages long, handwritten. It must have been okay, since they passed me."

His father's expression changed—part smile, part frown. "I don't care if you passed or not. I want to know the truth."

The truth?

Impossible.

Because the truth meant telling him about the caller.

And the caller only made sense if he told his dad about the picture the caller now had.

And there was no way that was ever going to happen.

The bullying, the mac and cheese, the suspension, getting grounded, the two-day course—he went through all of it to keep people from knowing about that picture.

But that wasn't the question.

What his father wanted to know is if he accepted responsibility for the things he had done to Connor Stark, and the answer to that was easy.

"I was . . . it was . . . all my fault. I'm . . . I'm sorry, Dad—"

Just not easy to say.

His father nodded and looked away. "Well . . ." After a quiet moment, he pointed to the screen and said, "There's that stupid robot again."

Eric watched the commercial, and when the game resumed, he shared his father's excitement for the interception and runback. For an hour and a half, they talked about amazing plays, overrated players, bad commercials, and the weather, neither one of them going anywhere near the reason why Eric would be spending the week at home. But it hung there in the room, and no matter how loud they cheered, he could hear a strange sadness in his father's voice.

He had never thought about his "relationship" with his parents. They were his parents, and that was all there was to it. Oh, sure, it was different from what his friends had, and they liked to say how they wished their parents were as cool as his, but Eric knew that that didn't mean anything — every kid said stuff like that, everybody else's parents somehow better than your own. Looking back, though, he wondered how he'd missed just how right his friends had been.

But things had changed, and it bothered him that he couldn't figure out exactly how.

Because if he couldn't figure out how things were different, he couldn't make them right again.

What he'd done to Connor Stark was wrong, no way

around it. But what he'd done to his parents was worse. The way his father had apologized to the principal, how his mother would tear up when she tried to talk to him? He felt like shit just thinking about it.

Then he'd think about the caller and the picture and he'd want to puke.

Well, nothing he could do about it now.

He'd done what he had to do.

And that girl — Shelly? — she was wrong. The caller would keep his end of the bargain, Eric was sure of it.

Or her end.

Whatever.

He was just glad it was over.

There was no way he could go through that again.

Sunday night, 9:30. Eric's phone rang.

He was sitting in his bed, reading *Travels with Charley* for English, one of the three books Ms. Salatel had assigned when they suspended him. In class they were reading *Of Mice and Men,* and he'd have to read that, too, writing the same essay as the others, plus a compare-and-contrast essay they didn't have to do. It was like that in all of his classes: piled-on work, part of his punishment.

The book was pretty good, which was a surprise, and he was so into it that he didn't notice that there was no caller ID number when he answered.

Then he heard the static.

"Hello, Eric."

He sat up. His left hand closed into a tight fist. He tried to picture a girl behind the booming baritone voice. Then he remembered that it was over, he'd done his part, it was time to let it go. He turned up the stereo in case his parents walked by, forced himself to take a slow, deep breath, and got right to it.

"Did you see the video?"

"Yes."

"It had four hundred hits before the school made me take it down."

"Closer to three hundred," the caller said.

"Yeah, well, still, that's a lot of hits for only being up a couple of hours."

Static.

"I used three servings of macaroni and cheese," Eric said, pacing the room, moving the call along. "And I waited until he looked up at me, just like you said to do."

Static.

"I got in big trouble for this, you know. They gave me a week's suspension, plus I had to go to this antibullying class."

Static.

"My parents are really pissed off."

Static.

"I'm probably grounded for the rest of the year."

Static.

"Look, I did what you said, so now —"

"You didn't follow my instructions."

Eric stopped. "Huh?"

"You didn't do what I told you to do."

"I did so," he said, his voice rising an octave. "I dumped a plate of mac and cheese on his head in the cafeteria. In front of everybody. That's what you said."

"There was more."

"Okay, okay, listen," he said, the words rushing together. "All right, yes, I skipped a couple of the days harassing him in school, but I had to. He was going to tell somebody, and then I would have gotten suspended before I could do the whole cafeteria thing."

"That's not it."

"You mean about YouTube? Hey, it got posted. You saw it yourself. I can't help it that the school made me take it down."

"No. Something else. Something important."

"Bullshit. I did everything you said."

Static.

"Tell me," Eric said. "What did I miss?"

"I said it had to be done on Thursday."

"I *did*," he said, mouth tight so he couldn't shout. "Last Thursday. First lunch. Around ten forty. You can see the cafeteria clock right on the video."

Static.

"What, you don't believe me? I can send you the letter the school sent my parents. It's got all the details."

"Not *that* Thursday," the caller said. "*This* Thursday."

"That's it? I'm a week early?"

"I was very specific as to when it had to be."

"Uh-uh," Eric said, shaking his head. "You never said it had to be this Thursday."

"I told you it had to —"

"You're crazy. You didn't tell me that."

Static.

"You never said a word about it being on a *specific* Thursday."

Static.

"And what difference does it make, anyway? It was a Thursday. It's the same thing."

Static.

"Oh, what, now you're not going to say anything?"

Static.

Eric waited.

Ten seconds.

Twenty.

Thirty.

He was about to hang up when the caller spoke.

"Do it again."

Eric froze.

"You were a week early," the caller said. "You'll have to do it all again."

"No way. I'm done. I did what you told me to do."

"You have no choice, Eric."

"We had a deal," he said, then he said it again, keeping his voice down, adding more, saying the things he'd been wanting to say since the first call, stringing the swear words tight together as he slammed his fist against his thigh, his face hot and his head pounding from deep inside.

He paused to catch his breath, the static roaring between them.

"I'm not doing it again," he said.

"Yes, you will. You'll do it again. You have to. Because if you don't, I'll send that picture to everyone you know," the caller said. "Starting with April."

The static faded in and out, then dropped off to nothing as the line went dead.

FOURTEEN

SHELLY WAS SITTING AT THE TABLE, MOVING SOGGY Cheerios around in the bowl, when Jeff came down the stairs and into the kitchen. He didn't jump when he finally noticed her, but for a flash of a second he had that look again, as if he was trying to place where he had seen this girl before. He turned on the water and let it run as he got a bag of Starbucks Blue Java out of the fridge. Shelly watched him scoop the grounds into a paper filter, watched his lips twitch as he worked out what to say, settling, as always, on the predictable.

"No school today?"

Shelly was tempted to say yes and leave it at that. It would be the answer he'd want to hear, because that would mean the conversation would be over and he could wait in silence for the coffee to brew. It would also mean that she wouldn't have to say anything to him, either, and that was always the right answer. But she was going to be home for the whole week — they would probably bump into each other a few more times, and that would mean more questions. Better to get a good multimorning reason out there first thing.

"I was suspended, remember?"

He tapped the top of the machine, prodding it to brew faster. "Oh, yeah," he said, either to himself or to Mr. Coffee.

Jeff had moved out right after Shelly was born.

Her parents had never divorced, but that was because they had never bothered to get married. She had vague memories of him stopping by over the years, but they were so random and disconnected that she could've imagined them, putting his face and grunted words on some other scrawny white guy's body. Real or not, the visits stopped years before her mother started seeing Aaron, a guy she worked with at Home Depot. When Aaron was offered an assistant manager's position at a new store, the three of them moved east, two hundred and twenty miles down the highway.

Aaron was okay. He was crazy about her mother and never looked at Shelly in that creepy way new stepfathers always did in the books she read. And he wasn't obsessed with being a "dad." If she wanted to talk to him, great — if not, oh well, he was cool with that, too. Without ever saying it, they had agreed to not make each other's lives difficult. No drama, no power plays, getting along because it was easier than not getting along.

For almost two years it was good, through the wedding and everything. It didn't even change when Luke came along, a whole month early.

Four months after that, though, everything was different.

"I suppose you're going to be hanging around the house all day," Jeff said, not bothering to disguise his disappointment.

Shelly was about to say yes, she'd be home, and that she'd try to stay in her room, when they both heard the upstairs toilet flush.

Company.

Who would it be this time?

Julie, the mall security guard who liked vodka with her morning coffee?

Lily-Ann, the one with the impossibly sweet southern drawl and the husband in Kuwait?

Iris, who didn't say anything at all?

The Thai woman, who had probably been very pretty many, many years ago?

Or a new friend who only needed a place to crash for the night?

What they saw in him she had no clue. Maybe there was something irresistible about short, skinny, thirty-five-year-old white guys with entry-level jobs and limited vocabularies that she wasn't old enough yet to understand and prayed to God she never would be.

What he saw in them — other than their low standards

—was a good question too, but not one that she was ever going to ask.

Shelly decided that it would be best if the mystery guest remained a mystery. She knew Jeff felt the same way.

"I was going to spend the day at the library," Shelly said, and when she saw the way Jeff's eyes lit up she added, "but I need money to get there and back. And to get something to eat."

Jeff reached for his wallet. "Twenty bucks enough?"

Upstairs, someone sang an Adele song, off-key but with heart.

Shelly smiled. "Make it forty."

As soon as Shelly flopped down in her usual seat at the back of the bus, a ringtone went off. She knew it had to be hers—there were no other passengers—but it was such a rare occurrence that she looked around, just to be sure. She took her phone out of her backpack, flipped it open, and saw the caller's number displayed on the screen. She didn't recognize the number, but since there *was* a number, she knew it wasn't going to be *that* caller. Then Shelly remembered Eric, the jock from the seminar, hit the button, and said hello.

But it wasn't him, either.

"Hi, Shelly? This is Fatima. I was in that class with you at the Community Center?"

"Yeah, I remember," Shelly said. "You were the one in the hijab."

"Wow, most people call it a headscarf."

"I guess I paid attention in social studies."

"Look, you're probably wondering why I'm calling you—"

"Actually, I'm wondering how you got my number."

"I got it from Ms. Owens after the session. I hope you don't mind."

"Well, to be honest—"

"It's just that I saw how you reacted, and I was kinda hoping we could talk."

Shelly sat up. "Reacted to what?"

"Remember when Ms. Owens was talking to the security guard about what some of the others—the ones who got dropped—wrote in their essays? She said something about this girl who got these phone calls?"

"Go on," Shelly said.

"When I was getting your number, I asked her about it, and Ms. Owens said that the girl was on these meds and was always hearing phones ringing."

"Fascinating. Why are you telling me this?"

"It's just that when Ms. Owens mentioned that girl to the guard, I don't know, you got all . . ."

"What are you trying to say?"

Fatima paused, and Shelly could hear her draw in a shaky breath. "I don't know why you're picking on people, but it's wrong and I—"

Shelly laughed. "You think *I'm* picking on people?"

"Yeah, I guess," Fatima said. "I mean, the way you acted was really weird, and it got me thinking that maybe—"

"I'm not picking on anybody. I swear," Shelly said, holding her hand up as if Fatima could see it.

"And the way you were staring down that guy in our group—"

"Eric?"

"Plus, in the parking lot? The way you were yelling at him?"

"We were talking."

"It sorta sounded like the voice on the phone, only not all changed and stuff—"

Shelly stopped. "What did you say?"

"—and the words were different, and you were shouting—"

"Okay, hold on."

"—so, not *exactly* like it, but with all the computer enhancements it could have—"

"Fatima, shut up for a second, will ya?"

"See? The way you're yelling? That's what made me think it was you."

Shelly held the phone away from her face, took a moment to breathe, pressed her thumbnail in deep, and tried again.

"Look, I'm sorry. It's just that you said you heard a voice —"

"The computerized one? Yeah, when I got the phone calls. That's why when I heard Ms. Owens talking about somebody getting a strange call, I looked up. And that's when I saw you acting all, you know . . ."

"Weird," Shelly said, finishing the thought. "When you got these phone calls, what did the caller say?" There was a long silence that served as an answer, then Shelly said, "I got those phone calls too."

"I doubt it," Fatima said. "I'm sure it wasn't *anything* like the calls I got."

"Macaroni and cheese?"

"Oh my god."

Shelly smiled. "What are you doing today?"

FIFTEEN

ERIC WAS BACK FROM THE GYM AND ABOUT TO SHOWER when the texts sent to his still-confiscated phone started coming in on his iPad.

The first one was from Yousef.

WTF?

Ten seconds later, there was one from Emma.

??????????

Then one from Tabitha.

CUTE!

Maya sent a stupid yellow smiley-face emoticon with an I-don't-get-it expression.

It was the fifth text, the one from Duane, that made his heart stop.

RULE #1: DON'T TAKE PICTURES WHEN YOU'RE STONED.

No.

His hand shook as he tried to get his fingers to obey, hitting the wrong keys, tapping on useless apps.

No, no, no, no, no —

He held his breath, waiting the two years it took for his stupid damn email account to open.

Please, no.

The same EarthLink account email, sent to him and to all 184 contacts on his phone.

The subject line read, ERIC HAMILTON, PHOTOGRAPHER.

Inside, no text, just a photo.

Oh, shit.

A black rectangle at the top, a rough white area in the middle, a dark brown bar along the bottom — and that was all.

His knees buckled, and he dropped to his bed, his stomach bunching up, a dull roar in his ears. He sat there, staring at the screen. Then his phone rang, and for a moment he wasn't sure what to do. On the sixth ring he answered, knowing already the voice he would hear.

"You have until Thursday. Then I send out the other photo."

For ten minutes, Eric sat on the edge of his bed, his heart pounding, his body numb, a little voice in his head droning on.

What the hell were you thinking?

It wasn't enough simply doing it. No, you had to go and document it.

For what?

To prove to yourself it really happened?

A souvenir?

As if you wouldn't remember it for the rest of your life.

Except you'd give anything now to forget it.

Damn.

There are probably laws about having a picture like that, even on your phone.

Swear you deleted it, *she had said.*

So you swore that you did.

It was gone now — deleted, dumped, erased, wiped clean.

Your copy, anyway.

The caller? She still has hers.

And if you don't do what she says, everybody you know will have a copy of their own.

Eric found the balled-up paper in the bottom of his backpack and punched in the number.

SIXTEEN

SHELLY LED THE WAY THROUGH THE GLASS DOOR. "I've got us booked in here for two hours, every day for a full week."

"We only need it till Thursday," Eric said, following her into the small room.

Fatima nodded, looping a shoulder strap of her backpack on the arm of one of the chairs, sliding the Jumbo Fun Time Sketch Pad! on the table. "After Thursday, it won't matter."

"Well, we'll keep the room reserved anyway," Shelly said. "In case we need a place to hide."

The six Theodore J. Marello Memorial Study Labs that split the reference area of the main library all had the same spartan features: floor-to-ceiling glass on both sides — which, the librarian reminded Shelly, allowed *everyone* to see *anything* that was going on — and regular walls between the study labs, lined with bulletin-board material to help with the soundproofing. The rooms were seldom used — the metal chairs were cold and hard, the lighting weak, and there were no outlets to plug into. But they were free, and there was a big-enough table, and even with all the glass it was still more private than meeting at Starbucks.

Fatima tore out a sheet of newsprint from the sketch pad and tacked it to the wall. "I guess we should start by telling each other all about ourselves."

"Guess again," Eric said.

"Yeah, let's not do that," Shelly said. "I'm not big on sharing."

"Fine. What do we do, then?"

Fatima and Eric both looked at Shelly, their eyebrows arched.

Shelly sighed and shook her head, suddenly in charge. "We all got the same call, right? Let's start there. Fatima, when did you get the *first* call?"

"Last Monday. Right after *Family Guy.* A rerun, obviously."

"Which one?" Eric asked.

"The one where Brian owes Stewie money."

"Best episode ever."

"Oh my god," Fatima said. "I was laughing *so* hard—"

"Fine, two thumbs up," Shelly said. "Can we stay focused here? What time was this masterpiece over?" She popped the cap off an orange marker and wrote WHEN on the paper. Under that, she put three bullet points.

Fatima glanced up at the ceiling. "Maybe nine?"

Shelly put *F 9* after the first bullet and *S 9:30* after the second.

"Looks like she started with me," Eric said. "I got my first call two weeks ago. Wednesday night, around ten. It sounded like a prank, so I hung up. Then he — sorry, *she* — called again a few minutes later. That's when she said, 'I know your secret.' But that time she hung up on me."

"Smart," Shelly said, adding Eric's details to the list. "Hanging up like that, she got in your head."

"I don't think so."

"Really? I bet you couldn't wait till that last call came. And don't worry, she got in all of our heads."

"I can't believe you hung up," Fatima said. "Weren't you even *curious?*"

He shrugged. "Not really. I mean, calling with that I-know-your-secret stuff? That's something you do when you're in fourth grade. You could say that to *anybody* and they'd freak."

"That's pretty much what I did," Fatima said. "I ended up just about begging her to tell me what she knew. And then, well, she did."

"I didn't have to beg," Eric said. "She called back, then sent me an email from a bogus EarthLink account."

"And something in the email proved she knew your secret?"

Eric nodded.

"All right, let's go there next." Below the bullet points, Shelly wrote *WHAT*.

"We're going to tell what our secret is? I don't think so," Eric said.

"Sorry, that's not what I meant," Shelly said. She crossed out *WHAT* and wrote *EVIDENCE*. "She's got something on each of us —"

"No kidding."

"— but it's gotta be something that's really obvious."

"If it was obvious, then it wouldn't be a secret."

Shelly ignored him. "Whatever it is she's got on each of us, it's gotta be self-evident."

Eric looked at her. "*Self-evident?* Can you just say what you mean?"

"No, hold on, I got it," Fatima said. "You're saying that whatever evidence she has, it has to be something that she doesn't have to explain to people. Right?"

Shelly closed her eyes and smiled. "Exactly."

Eric knocked on the table. "Why?"

"Because she's not gonna want to be there to have to explain it to them," Fatima said. "She just wants people to look at it or read it or whatever and know right away what the big secret is."

Eric took a second, then nodded. "Okay. Go on."

"For me — and this is all I'm going to tell you — she's got information." Shelly wrote the word on the paper.

"Vague much? Everything is information," Fatima said.

Shelly played with the marker as she thought it through, pulling the cap off and snapping it back in place. "She knows something about me," she finally said. "Is that good enough?"

Eric waved his hand, moving her along.

"A book," Fatima said. "She has a book of mine."

"Like a journal?"

"Sorta. But not really. Can you just put down 'book' for now?"

Shelly added it to the list, glancing at Eric as she wrote. "Your turn."

"I don't see the point of this," he said. "How can knowing what she has help us figure out who it is?"

"It might not," Shelly said. "But we don't have much to go on, do we? It's a piece of the puzzle, that's all. Maybe an important piece, maybe not. Later it might make all the difference. Or none. Look, you don't have to be specific. I wasn't. Is it bigger than an X-box?"

He sighed and rubbed the hint of stubble on his chin. "It's a picture."

"A painting, a photograph . . . ?"

"A photo."

"Digital?"

"Yeah," he said, dropping his hands hard onto the arms of the metal chair. "A digital photograph. Happy?"

"Yes, thank you," Shelly said, writing it all down. "Now the harder question. How'd she get it?"

"No frickin' clue," Eric said.

Fatima tilted her head. "I thought you said she took a picture of you."

"She *has* a picture. She didn't take it."

"So she wasn't there?"

Eric looked down at the table, his hand coming up to cover his mouth as he smiled. "No, she wasn't there."

"You sure?"

"I'm sure," he said, his eyes shifting back and forth.

Shelly watched him, nodding, then said, "So I'm guessing that you know who took the picture and you're positive that whoever took it didn't give it to the girl who's calling us. Am I close?"

"Close enough, yeah."

"Since it's digital, she might have hacked into your computer—"

"It was on my phone," he said. "You can't hack into a phone."

"Yes, you can," Fatima said. "My cousin? Hassan? He's, like, a computer expert. I've heard him say that there's ways to do it but it's really complex. You gotta be linked into a network or something."

"Okay, that's one way the caller could have gotten the picture," Shelly said, adding it to the paper. "Did you loan your phone to a friend or something?"

He laughed. "They have their own."

"Fine. Ever lose your phone anywhere?"

"No, I've always got it. My mother has it now, but before that, I always had it."

"You *never* left it anywhere accidentally, even for a minute?"

"Well, yeah, sure. But it was never more than, I don't know, five minutes? She couldn't get to it that quick."

"You'd be surprised at what can happen in five minutes," Shelly said, more to herself than to the others. "So it's possible she stole it. How long for doesn't matter."

"My book got stolen," Fatima said. "She took it out of my locker."

"Excellent. Now we know she goes to your school," Eric said.

Shelly shook her head. "No, it only means that she got into the school building. You have to wear a uniform or something?"

"No," Fatima said, making a face. "It's just Springtown. A regular high school."

"So any girl could walk around there and nobody would notice."

"Yeah, probably."

"And do you always lock your locker every time?"

"No one does. We got, like, two minutes between classes. You don't want to spend half of it dialing in the combination. You close it almost all the way and it's good enough."

Eric looked at Shelly. "What about you? How'd she get this . . . *information?*"

"She didn't have to break in, if that's what you mean," Shelly said. "I don't know how she found it."

"Could I find it?"

"No," Shelly said, and before Eric could ask another question, she said, "We know more or less what she has, and for you guys, how she got it. All that's left is to figure out who she is."

"*Who she is* is a psycho," Eric said.

"That's a what," Shelly said, "and given some of the girls I've met, it doesn't narrow it down much."

Fatima said, "Let's make a list of everyone we know and see who we all know in common."

"That's crazy," Eric said. "You know how long that would take?"

"True, but it's the right idea," Shelly said, "and there's an easier way. We each make a list of the things we do and compare that — say, like, sports, church, community service, clubs . . . that kind of stuff."

"It's the same thing you said the other day in the parking lot."

"You mean the same thing she shouted," Fatima said.

"Yeah, she *was* loud."

"I could hear her way back at the building. It shook the glass."

"Tell me about it. I was standing right next to her."

Shelly listened as they talked about her as if she wasn't there. After what she went through at her last school, she was used to it. When they finished, she smiled at them and said, "We've got three days. Less than that. Then everyone learns the one thing we don't want them to know. Now, unless you've got a better idea, this is where we start."

Three hours later, they walked out of the library. Eric was smiling when he said, "Well, *that* was a waste of time."

"No, we just didn't solve it today, that's all. We'll try again tomorrow. I'm sure we'll figure it out."

"I like your attitude," Fatima said.

Shelly smiled. "Thanks."

"I think you're *crazy,* and I think we're *totally* screwed, but I still like your attitude."

Eric thumped one of the rubber bands that held the rolled-up sheets of newsprint. "What should I do with this stuff?"

"There's no way I could bring that home," Fatima said. "*Way* too many questions." She waved at a silver SUV in the parking lot. "There's my mom. Same time tomorrow?"

"Absolutely."

"Sure," Eric said. "I've got nothing else to do."

Fatima jogged out and climbed into the passenger seat, leaning over to kiss her mother on the cheek as the SUV drove away.

"How much you wanna bet her horrible secret is that she held some guy's hand?"

"That's a stereotype," Shelly said. "Just because she's a Muslim doesn't mean it's like that."

"Fine. How much you wanna bet?"

"I'm a good Catholic girl. The only gambling I'm allowed to do is bingo. Come on, walk me over to the bus stop."

"I can give you a ride home."

"Thanks, but I like the bus," Shelly said, starting down the sidewalk. "That's where I do my best thinking."

He fell in step next to her, slowing his pace to match her shorter legs. "You think we're going to figure out who it is?"

"Honestly? No. Fatima's right, we're screwed."

"So why bother?"

She shrugged. "What else are we supposed to do?

Roll over and wait for it without even trying to save ourselves?"

"It's an option."

"I'd rather fail trying than succeed at not trying."

"That made no sense."

"Most things don't," she said. "Especially this. I'm telling you, it's totally pissing me off. Don't laugh — I'm serious." She glanced over at him. "Tell me you're not pissed."

"Definitely."

"And scared?"

He hummed, then said, "A little, I guess."

"That's it? Just a little?"

"What do you want me to say? That I think about it all the time? That I'm up all night, puking 'cuz I'm so afraid of what could happen next?"

"I would if I were you."

"You worry about yourself," he said, balancing the rolled-up paper on the end of a finger. "I'm doing just fine."

She watched him as they walked, his hand steady, his eyes wide, the tip of his tongue poking out between his lips as he concentrated on keeping the paper upright. It was an act — she was sure of it — but he was playing it off pretty good. Shelly checked her phone. The number twenty-four bus was three minutes away. Just enough time. She closed her phone and said, "Has she seen it?"

He kept his focus on the paper. "Who?"

"Your girlfriend."

"Don't have one."

"Okay, your ex-girlfriend. Has she seen it?"

The paper wobbled. "Has she seen what?"

"The naked picture you took of her."

His finger twitched, and the paper tube dropped sideways. He grabbed for it with his left hand and missed. It bounced around on the sidewalk, and he stooped to pick it up. "I don't know what you're talking about."

"Really? We're gonna have to do this? You pretending you don't know what I mean and me having to keep saying it?"

Eric whacked the paper against a light pole. The roll bent a bit, a sooty scuff below a rubber band to mark where it hit.

"It wasn't hard to figure out," Shelly said. "You said it was a picture, and it was on your phone, so odds are it was you who took it. And when Fatima asked if the caller was there when the picture was taken? You had that look guys get when they're talking about sex."

He shook his head. "That's just stupid."

"Trust me — girls know. When you're with your friends and some cheerleader walks down the hall? We see the look you get."

"I don't get *some look*—"

"Not just *you*," she said. "All guys. And that's the look you had on your face when Fatima was asking you about the picture. Now, if it was a picture of you having sex with another guy—"

"*What?*"

"—you wouldn't have smirked like that. That's because you're not openly gay—"

"*I'm not gay at all!*"

"—and if it was a picture of you and another guy having sex—"

"*Stop saying that.*"

"—you wouldn't have shown *any* emotion, since you'd be trying to hide how you really felt. But you had that sex look, so I figure it was you and a girl."

"This is insane."

"And you have to be able to see her face in the picture. Or a tattoo. Something that would make her easy to identify. Oh, and it's not just *any* girl. It's somebody you care about. If it was only some quick hookup, you wouldn't be so worried about the picture getting out. If it did, you'd be like, 'Yeah, I hit it, no big deal.'"

"*No.* I'm not *like* that."

"Sure you're not," Shelly said, digging through her backpack for her bus pass. "Anyway, that's how I figured that the caller has a picture of your ex-girlfriend naked." She looked up at him and smiled. "Right?"

He started to say something, stopped, started again, then looked away.

"At least that explains why you were so willing to dump mac and cheese on some kid," Shelly said. "If I had a boyfriend and he took a naked picture of me and that picture got out? His life would be over. I mean it. I would destroy him."

"Gee, thanks. That makes me feel better."

"It was a shitty thing to do, you know."

"I'm not disagreeing," he said.

"Don't worry, you're not the only one around here who wants to crawl under a rock and disappear."

"Whatever it is you got, it can't be worse than mine."

She laughed at that.

Eric tapped her arm with the paper roll. "You wanna swap problems? I'd rather have to deal with your secret than mine."

"I seriously doubt that."

"Oh, I get it now," he said, slapping his forehead. "You're pregnant."

"I'm a virgin," she said. "And that's no big secret." She laughed again and turned away as the number twenty-four bus pulled toward the curb.

"Wait, I still want to swap," Eric said, raising his voice to be heard over the bus's hissing air brakes and clattering door. "Unless, of course, if you killed somebody."

Halfway into the bus, Shelly stopped, leaned back, and glared at him, her smile gone, her face hard, her dark brown eyes, black now, staring into his.

Then she stepped inside, the doors snapped shut, and the bus pulled away.

Eric's mouth hung open as he stood alone on the sidewalk, the paper tube slipping from his fingers.

SEVENTEEN

THE RULE IN THE EL-RAFIE HOUSE WAS THAT WHEN YOU got home from school, you sat at the kitchen table and did your homework until it was time for dinner or prayers, whichever came first. That night it would be dinner.

Fatima sat in her father's chair at the head of the table. At the other end, Haytham was busy solving for X, and halfway between them — and taking up the most room — Alya worked on coloring inside the lines. At the stove, her mother stirred the pot of pasta sauce, overloaded with onions like everything she made.

Fatima flipped the pages of her history book, the centuries flying by, her mind miles away. She had a full week to complete the work her teachers had sent home for her to do while she was suspended. It would take a couple of hours, tops, to get it all done. There was no need to rush.

Besides, after Thursday, what happened in school wouldn't matter much anymore. Fatima plopped her chin in her hand and looked around the room.

There was Haytham, his hair a mess, pushing his glasses up his nose again and again.

And Alya, her little fingers balled up around the busted crayon.

Her mother, hijab off, her hair pulled back into a long black ponytail.

And any minute now, the door opening, her father coming in, saying what he said every day he came home to find his family waiting.

Alhamdillah.

Thanks be to God.

Right at that moment, it was all still the same.

Like it had been for years.

Like she always thought it would be, forever.

She missed it already.

She looked down at the textbook — notes in pen and pencil, squirreled between lines, in the whitespace around charts, across maps and over pictures of kings, presidents, wars, and ruins. Like every book she owned.

It had started back in preschool, where she earned huge gold stars for her neat letters, mastering the whole alphabet before the rest of the class was up to *E*. Then the words came, and sentences, the ideas getting longer and more complex, her handwriting becoming more precise, the praise more addicting. By third grade, she didn't need to be reminded to write things down, and she never lost points for not writing enough. She earned check-pluses in computer class, touch-typing coming easy, but given the option, it was always pen and paper over a keyboard. Around sixth grade, it became obsessive. No thought was too small to record, no space too tiny for more notes. At the end of every school year her parents would get a bill for the textbooks that she'd ruined, but the straight A's and high-honor-roll certificates covered the cost, her peculiar habit a small price to pay for success.

Then she went one book too far.

Her mother rapped the wooden spoon against the edge of the pot. "You two, clean up your things, then go wash your hands. Fatima, stir this while I strain the spaghetti."

"It'll be fine, Mom," Fatima said. "Just let it simmer a bit."

"Suddenly you know how to cook? Come, stir," her mother said, holding out the spoon.

Fatima sighed with dramatic flair and took her place at the stove. Her brother and sister cleared the table, then raced down the hall to the bathroom.

"So, tell me about your day," her mother said, as if it was any old day and not the first day of the only suspension an El-Rafie had ever earned since before the time of the Prophet.

"I did some research for my earth science project. It's on soil erosion?"

"Are you asking me or telling me? You need to speak properly if you expect people to take you seriously."

"My most excellent project, it is on the glorious process that geologists call soil erosion," Fatima said, nailing the clipped tones of her mother's accent.

"Don't get smart, young lady."

Fatima faked a smile and let it go.

Then her mother said, "That girl and boy with you at the library. Who were they?"

"I told you. They were in the tolerance-awareness program with me. Eric and Shelly."

"Quite a coincidence that you were all at the library at the same time."

Good point, Fatima thought, but said, "Not really. Their parents told them the same thing you and Dad told me. This isn't a vacation: it's punishment."

A cloud of steam rose up from the sink as her mother emptied the pot of spaghetti into the strainer. "What did they do at the library?"

"School stuff, I guess. I didn't ask."

"You be careful around them."

"What do you mean?"

"You know exactly what I mean."

"Oh, *please,*" Fatima said, laughing. "They're not *evil* or anything."

"Yes, I forgot. The best children get suspended most."

"Mom, they made a mistake, that's all. Just like me."

"No," her mother said, shaking the strainer. "Not just like you. They can afford to make mistakes. They can afford to get suspended. It's not the same for you."

Because you're a Muslim. It was assumed — always and with everything — the reality that shaped all other realities, the ultimate answer to any question.

Why can't I?

Why should I?

Why do I have to?

Because you're a Muslim.

Simple, clear, comforting, and true.

For as long as Fatima could remember, it had been enough.

Then it wasn't.

"People see your name, see your hijab, they assume the worst. *Wallah,*" her mother said, eyes heavenward, her hand on her heart. "It is so, always."

Not always, Fatima thought. *Sometimes, maybe even often, but not always.*

Her mother set the strainer in the sink and leaned against her daughter, her arm slipping around her tiny waist. Fatima felt the squeeze, heard the choked-back sigh, and kept her eyes on the spoon as she stirred the sauce.

"Oh, *habibti.*"

My baby.

She knew there would be tears in her mother's eyes, and she knew what would happen if she saw them. Fatima kept stirring.

"Why, *habibti?* Why?"

A tighter squeeze.

"Calling that poor girl names like that . . ."

Another choppy sigh.

"Your father and I, we try our best . . ."

Fatima sniffed, rubbing the back of her hand against her nose.

"Is this the way we raised you, to treat people like that?"

Fatima swallowed hard, whispered, "No, Mom."

"Oh, *habibti*. Why?"

Fatima thought —

I had no choice.

Because if I didn't, you and Daddy and Aunty Nisreen and Aunty Heba, Aunty Rehma and Uncle Ahmed, all the El-Rafies and all the Lobads, all the people at the Islamic Center, the families back in Egypt and the ones in London, everyone whose name and email address I had handwritten — compulsively, ridiculously — in the Hello Kitty address book you bought for me when I was twelve, all of you would know what none of you can know.

What she said, in a voice so low her mother didn't hear, was, "I'm sorry I hurt you."

The front door opened and a deep, laughing voice said, *"Alhamdillah."* Haytham and Alya raced down the hall and through the kitchen to be the first to hug Daddy.

"Promise me this," her mother said, giving her one last squeeze. "Promise me you'll never shame your family again."

Fatima closed her eyes. "I promise," she said, knowing it was already broken.

EIGHTEEN

EYES ON THE SCREEN, ERIC HEADED THE CORNER KICK from Ronaldo into the goal, putting Real Madrid up by three against Chelsea with ten minutes left to play, saying, "And — again — the crowd goes wild."

Through the headset, Duane said, "That's because the refs didn't call the offsides. Again."

"Spoken like a true loser."

"I do my winning on a real team," Duane said.

"Hilarious."

"What? Too soon?"

The screen showed the goal again in slow motion.

"Not too soon to bury you," Eric said.

The players were gathering at midfield for the restart when Eric heard the kitchen phone ring and, a moment later, his mother shouting his name, saying it was for him. Before, he wouldn't have bothered, let his mom take a message. But that was before. "Gotta go," he said as he logged out, then ran down the stairs.

"Hey, E-man. How's it hanging?"

Garrett.

April's brother.

That was one call he wasn't expecting.

"Hey," Eric said. "'Zup?"

"Need a hand moving some furniture. You busy?"

Later, when Eric thought about it, he realized it made no sense. Garrett lived in the dorm and it already had furniture. And if he needed help lifting stuff, there were plenty of guys there — guys who were much bigger than a high school junior. And Garrett knew a lot of big guys. But that was later, and when Garrett backed his Toyota out of the driveway, Eric wedged between two of those big guys in the back seat, he didn't think anything about it.

Garrett shouted a thanks-dude over the pounding music, and Eric shouted a no-problem, then nobody said anything as they made their way out of the subdivision, onto one street, then another, then a highway, then an off-ramp and another street, eventually turning onto a county road that led away from town. The front yards got bigger the farther they went, the houses set farther from the road, the standard-size suburban homes replaced by McMansions, then older farmhouses, then trailer parks, then lone trailers and low ranch houses every mile or so. They'd been on the road twenty minutes when Garrett turned off the music.

"So, Eric, how's soccer going?"

It wasn't.

The coach had been there when the principal had

suspended him, letting Eric know just how disappointed he was, telling Eric how he'd let the whole team down, how he'd tarnished the image of every athlete at the school. He talked about second chances, sure, and how next season Eric could start fresh, earn his way back to first string where he belonged, but that for this season he'd have to cheer his former teammates on from the stands. Three years ago, Garrett had been the team captain, and he kept in touch with the coach, so Eric was sure he knew all the details.

"I got kicked off the team."

"Bummer," said the big guy to his left.

"Yeah, bummer," said the one on the right.

"Sorry to hear that," Garrett said, not sounding sorry at all. "You staying in shape? Running, hitting the gym, that kind of stuff?"

"It's only been a couple of days."

"You'd be surprised at how fast you'll get outta shape if you don't keep at it," Garrett said. "My advice is to set yourself up a training regimen. Do something every day, like you were still on the team. Weights, cardio. Mix it up. And stretching. Don't forget to stretch."

"I won't, thanks."

"I'm serious, Eric. You get outta shape, you'll regret it. I'm just trying to help, right, guys?"

The guy in the front nodded and there were mumbled agreements from right and left.

Out the window, telephone poles caught in the headlights raced past, and there were hints of empty farm fields.

It was quiet for a mile, then Garrett said, "So, it's been, like, what, two months since you and April broke up?"

And then it clicked.

The call, the big guys, the long ride.

"Something like that." He tried to shrug, but his shoulders were boxed in by the thick arms of his fellow backseat passengers.

From the left, "That sucks."

From the right, "Yeah."

"You guys get in a big fight?"

"No, not really," Eric said, keeping his answers short.

"Did she do something stupid?"

"No, nothing like that."

"Because people can do stupid things."

"Yeah, I suppose."

"Even people you think you know. They can surprise you with how stupid they can be." Garrett adjusted the rearview mirror. His eyes appeared to float in the cloudless sunset sky. "Take you, for instance. I thought I knew you pretty well. I thought you were cool. It didn't seem to bother you that I was gay, that all of my friends were gay—"

"*Most* of your friends," the big guy up front said, smiling as he punched Garrett in the arm.

"Fine, most. The point here, Eric, is that you fooled me. See, I would have bet good money that you'd never pick on some kid just because you thought he looked a bit on the gayish side. Or that you'd use all those nasty words—"

"It's not what you think," Eric started to say before he was elbowed in the ribs.

"Careful, Eric. My friends are not as understanding as I am. You see, I know how a guy's brain works. Straight or gay, it doesn't matter. We'll do just about anything to get laid. And if that means lying and pretending you're one thing when you're another? Well, we've all been there, right?"

The guy up front nodded. "That's the truth."

"And speaking of places where we've been," Garrett said, slowing down, easing the car to the side of the road. "You ever been out here?"

Eric glanced out the side window. "I don't know. Maybe."

The car rocked to a stop.

Garrett put it in park, undid his safety belt, and turned to face Eric.

"What you did to that kid with the macaroni and

cheese? You confused me. See, I really thought that you got it, that you understood why all my gay-lez-tranny kumbaya preaching was so important. And — spoiler alert — I thought you were cool. Well, you sure played me."

Eric wanted to look away, but knew it wouldn't be good.

"But you know what? That's life, right? In some way, we all get picked on and we all pick on others. The circle jerk of life. Now, do I *like* what you did? Of course not. But that's not why we're here today. No, see, what pissed me off — I mean *really* pissed me off — is how you hurt April."

"April? It happened after we broke up. It had nothing to do with us."

Garrett grit his teeth. "Maybe not, but she was in love with you, shithead. I don't know why, but she was. And then you go and do something like that? First guy she ever falls for turns out to be an asshole, bastard, lying prick? How do you think *that* makes her feel?"

Eric felt his stomach drop.

She was in love with you.

Was.

As in not now.

As in never again.

"Pay attention, little man," Garrett said, his finger an inch from Eric's face. "You ever do *anything* to hurt my sister again, and I will hurt you. Do you understand?"

Eric nodded.

"I'm sorry, I didn't quite get that," Garrett said, flicking the tip of Eric's nose.

"I understand," Eric said.

"Understand *what?*"

"If I do anything to hurt April, you'll hurt me."

Garrett smiled and looked around at his friends. "See? He's not *that* stupid." Then he looked back at Eric. "How fast can you run?"

"Run?"

"Yeah, how long would it take you to run, say, two miles?"

"I . . . I'm not sure . . ."

Garrett checked the clock on the dashboard. "Could you do it in under fifteen minutes? In what you're wearing?"

"I don't know. If I had to, I guess."

"Here's why I ask. About two miles up this road there's this service area. Gas station, little store. Know what I mean? Well, this service area, it's also the final stop on the bus line. Or the first, actually, if you lived out here. Anyway, the last bus heading back into town pulls out from that station in seventeen minutes."

"Sixteen minutes," the guy up front said. "It just changed."

"Sorry, sixteen minutes. And the next one isn't until five-something in the morning. You miss this one . . ." He shook his head, and the other passengers laughed. Then Garrett snapped his fingers, and the big guy to Eric's right opened the door and climbed out.

"I know you have to run," Garrett said, "but before you go, do I need to remind you how stupid it would be to mention my name when you're explaining your way out of this one?"

Eric raised his head and looked Garrett in the eyes.

Part of him wanted to say something smart like "Thanks for the lift" or "Now who's gonna carry the piano?"

Another part was ready with every variation of every swear word he knew.

A part of him — small, but there — was scared and didn't want to get out of the car.

But the biggest part of him knew he deserved it.

And if the picture ever got out and everybody saw it — and everybody *would* see it, too, emailing it and posting it and printing out copies and passing them around, everybody getting a good, long look, April dying a thousand deaths with every knowing smirk — if that happened, he'd deserve what he'd get then, too. People — the good ones, anyway — would be on her side, their hearts breaking for her even if they did sneak a peek. They'd play it off, pretend it never happened. But they'd never forget. And they'd never forget who was to blame.

"No, it's cool," Eric said as he slid out of the seat, stepping to the side so the big guy could get back in.

Garrett pulled away, then yanked the wheel for a quick U-turn. He rolled down the window and smiled at Eric. "Don't forget to stretch," he said, and drove off back down the flat, empty road.

NINETEEN

"*GOD IS GOOD*," FATHER JOE SHOUTED INTO THE MICRO-
phone, his smile bright in the early-morning gloom.

Nothing.

He held his arms wide, looking out at the dozen or so
people scattered among the church's pews, waiting for a
reply. They kept him waiting.

Shelly wondered how many more weeks he'd attempt
that call-and-response thing before finally giving up.
When he had tried it the other morning, the old people
had glanced around at each other, then did the courteous
thing and acted as if it never happened. Today they just
ignored him. Shelly imagined what it was like at Father
Joe's church in South Sudan — everyone shouting back,
the tin roof rattling with their joyous response, the spirit
of the Lord filling the whole congregation with contagious
excitement, a sea of black hands reaching together to
Heaven. But here, in this suburban church in this part of
America? Nothing. They stood there, waiting silently for
him to continue.

"*All the time,*" Father Joe said, smile undiminished, his
arms bouncing a bit, inviting participation.

Nothing.

Shelly would have liked to believe that the people were quiet because it was still so early — 7:30 on a Tuesday morning — but she knew that if every pew had been filled, if there were people lined along the back wall and the choir loft packed like it was Christmas, it would have been just as quiet. But he kept at it.

What was it that Father Caudillo used to say? *A stone doesn't have to speak to be moved.*

The priest raised his arms a notch higher and drew in a deep breath, closing his eyes as he tried again.

"All the time . . ."

She drew in a deep, shouting breath. "All the time . . ."

Okay, so she didn't shout it. At best it was a whisper in the cavernous church, but she said it, one little voice for them all.

Father Joe's smile grew. *"God is good!"*

"God is good," Shelly said, louder this time, but far from loud.

The priest opened his eyes and looked out on his congregation. "The mass has ended," he said, clipping the ends off each word. "Go in peace to love and serve the Lord."

The remaining parishioners mumbled something in unison, then one by one they made their way out of the church.

Shelly stayed.

She sat down, then slid her butt forward to rest the back of her head on the hard wooden pew. It was too cold in the church to sleep, but it was quiet, which seemed like enough.

She'd been awake since five, when her father and a guest had giggled and stumbled their way up the stairs and into his bedroom. Shelly managed to get dressed and out of the house before the squeaking started.

For the thousandth time, she considered her options.

Moving back in with her mother and Aaron wasn't one of them.

They had moved again right after it had happened, so it wouldn't be like she'd be in the same house, with that same room and all the same memories that would come with it. A new house might mean a new start, a fresh beginning. But she knew her mother would never let that happen. The thing was, Shelly couldn't blame her. Invite a monster into your new home? Don't be stupid. Even before the police had arrived that night, before her mother had learned what she had done, Shelly knew she wouldn't be able to sleep in that house anymore.

There was an aunt who lived on a farm in Alsask, a speck of a town somewhere in Saskatchewan. Shelly had been there when she was in third grade, and she remembered enough about the place to know that *that* wasn't an option either.

Uncle Dave and Aunt Robin were in the navy, so that was out, and her grandparents lived in a retirement community that had a strict no-one-under-sixty rule. She hadn't tried contacting them and assumed they liked it that way.

There were relatives on her father's side too, but he was considered the successful one of the Meyer family, so there was no reason to even look there.

She had had friends before she had moved across the state with her mom and Aaron, but that was years ago, and she hadn't exactly kept in touch with any of them. She had a hard time making friends as it was, and the few that possibly almost considered her a friend back then stopped calling the night the police cars arrived.

Running away was an option. She could live in a homeless shelter or on the streets or find a nice gang to join, and she was sure she'd make it a good two, three days before freaking out.

The truth was, she was a lonely, friendless fifteen-year-old introvert with a father who pretended she didn't exist, a mother who no doubt wished it was true, and a past she needed to escape.

And — she was doing it.

Slowly, one day at a time, like the bumper sticker said. Creating a new life, a new image, a new self, burying the old one under eye makeup and hair dye. Every forced smile cracking the ice, letting real smiles spread, every choreographed conversation inching her closer to a time when she could talk without thinking, without worrying she'd slip up and say something scary, writing a new future to go with her new past.

So damn close to making it happen, to making it be the truth.

Then the caller and her threat to take it all away.

Her anger made her laugh.

"I know, I know," Father Joe said as he walked down the aisle. "I meant to say that the hymn was a *folk in A major,* but it came out wrong. Do you think that anyone noticed?"

"No, your accent's too thick for anyone to notice anything," Shelly said. It was true, his accent did make English sound like a foreign language, yet that "folk in A" line had come through no problem, especially when he said it over and over. It was the shocked gasps from the old people that had made it so funny.

Father Joe took a seat in the row ahead, turning sideways to see her, his arm resting on the back of the pew. "Thank you for responding to my call during the service."

"I thought you could use a little help."

"It is so simple. I say, 'God is great,' then everyone says 'God is great.' Very common."

"Not here. Try the Baptist church down the road."

"Was there more participation at your St. Mark's church?"

"No, not really," Shelly said, impressed that he had remembered anything from their short conversation. "I think if people shouted out like that, Father Caudillo might not have liked it."

"Father Tony?" He clapped his hands, his already big smile somehow growing bigger. "Oh, no, Father Tony would most *definitely* not like it one bit."

"You know him?"

The priest waved to the custodian, who looked annoyed that there were still people hanging around. "I know Father Coly, who is from Senegal, and he in turn knows Father Tony."

"So you *don't* know him."

"Not myself personally, no. But is that not often the way? *A* knows *B*, *B* knows *C*, thusly *A* knows of *C*."

"Math's not really my thing," she said, checking the time on her phone as she pulled a bus schedule from her coat pocket. It would be hours before the library opened, but there was a Starbucks nearby, and that would do.

"It is elementary, Miss Shelly. You know of someone you have never met, thanks be to your mutual friends and random acquaintances. And people you do not know and have never met find you through these same connections."

Shelly froze.

"For instance, this is how I come to know Father Tony—"

She stared hard at nothing.

"—and how Father Coly comes to know Bishop Kussala—"

Pieces falling into place.

"—and how Bishop Kussala comes to know Sister Margaret Mary—"

The bus schedule slipping from her fingers and onto the floor.

"—and how Sister Margaret Mary comes to ..." The priest paused and leaned in. "Are you all right, Miss Shelly?"

"She doesn't know me."

"Oh, I think not. Sister Margaret Mary lives in Ghana. But that being the case—"

"She knows Heather," Shelly said, her voice flat and low as she talked it through. "And the only reason Heather knows me is that we go to the same school."

"Miss?"

Shelly started to smile. "It's not me she's after. It's Heather. And it's not Eric or Fatima, either. It's them."

"Are you all right, miss?"

"It was never about *us*. It's about *them*," Shelly said,

jumping to her feet, stumbling her way out of the pew. "*They're* the connection."

She pulled on her black Komor Kommando hoodie as she ran down the aisle. Behind her, Father Joe shouted an accent-thick blessing through his booming laugh.

TWENTY

ERIC LEANED BACK, BALANCING THE LIBRARY CHAIR ON two legs. "I'm not saying I don't believe you—"

"Are you sure? Because that's what it sounds like to me."

He took a breath. "I'm only saying, I don't see what difference it makes."

"Seriously? You don't see how important this clue is?"

"Not really, no."

"You've got to be kidding. It's *obvious*."

"Well, obviously it's not."

She looked across the table to Fatima, who was already scribbling away in her notebook. "You get it, right?"

"The first part, yes, about the caller not knowing us. Why it's important, not so much."

"And we don't know if that part's even true," Eric said.

Shelly ran her left hand through her hair. Her right hand was on her lap, and she stabbed her stubby thumbnail into the side of her index finger, holding the outburst back. Instead she said, "It's my fault. I'm not explaining myself very good."

"You got that right."

Another stab. "Let me try again." She unrolled a sheet of paper, using her phone to hold down one end and a paperback to hold the other, then she drew three intersecting circles on the page.

Fatima perked up. "Ooooh, a Venn diagram. Love 'em."

"Yesterday we were looking for a person that we all knew in common. Somebody in this space here."

"You mean an element within the subset of S union F union E," Fatima said, leaning over to label the circles with their names and shade the spot. "And you'd write the equation like this, with an upside-down *U* for *union*." She paused and read the looks they were giving her. "Sorry, math-geek genes run deep in my family."

Shelly tapped the shaded area where the three circles crossed. "We thought the person we were looking for would be in that spot. Like somebody I knew from church who was also somebody you knew from, I don't know—"

"Soccer," Eric said.

"Okay, soccer. Who was also someone Fatima knew from, say, her neighborhood. Make sense?"

"But we didn't find anyone," Fatima said. "There were a few people I knew that Eric *maybe* knew from sports, and there was that one girl from his school who had a job near my uncle's store, and you only had, what, like, ten names on your list?"

"I just moved here this summer."

"Still, you'd think you'd know more than ten people —"

"Fine, whatever," Shelly said, changing the discussion with a flick of her hand. "The point is that we didn't find anyone in common with all three of us. But we were looking at it wrong. It's not *us* that has a person in common, it's them."

"And them — I mean *they* — are the ones the caller told us to pick on?"

"Exactly. They each have something in common with her."

Fatima looked at the Venn diagram. "Yeah, but that doesn't mean that the three victims have anything in common with each other. Their connection to the caller could be something unique to each one of them."

"It's possible," Shelly said. "But since all three of the victims were getting the same treatment, I believe all of them — the victims and the caller — have one thing in common."

"You believe," Eric said, the doubt clear in his voice.

"It holds up logically," Fatima said. "To a point, anyway."

Eric crossed his arms. "So what you're saying is that to solve our problem, all we have to do is figure out everything that three people have in common with each other so we can find a fourth person."

"That's it."

He smiled at her. "Three people we barely know. Who hate us. And who we can't even talk to if we wanted—"

"To find a *fourth* person," Fatima said, "who you're suggesting none of us have ever met."

"You guys are making it sound harder than it is."

"Harder? I don't see how it could *be* harder."

"He's right," Fatima said. "I mean, what do I know about Katie?"

"Who?"

"The girl I was supposed to go after. Katie Schepler."

"Supposed to? You didn't do anything to her?"

"I tried. Turns out she's a lot tougher than she looks. She punches like a guy," Fatima said, making a balled-up shape that was nothing like a fist. "Of course, I got in more trouble than she did."

Shelly nodded. "Because you're a Muslim."

"God, you sound like my mother. No, I got in more trouble because I started it. What I was trying to say is that I don't know anything about her."

"I don't know much about that Stark kid. Connor. The one I dumped the plate on. I didn't even know he was in my school."

"And I didn't know anything about Heather Herman, either. But still we all figured out enough to know who to go after." She looked at Fatima. "Where'd you look?"

"Where else? Facebook," Fatima said.

"Me too. And that's where we start again."

"No way," Eric said. "I hear they can check to see who's been looking at your profile. I go to his page and I'm screwed."

"I'll go instead," Fatima said. "And you can go to the one for Shelly, and Shelly can go to the one for me."

Eric thought about it. "What if they're all blocked now, or restricted to friends or something?"

Shelly pushed her chair away from the table. "Only one way to find out."

Fatima bumped open the glass door of the study room, a small stack of papers in her hands.

"You print out his whole Facebook life?"

"Maybe," Fatima said. "I thought I hit 'print page,' but I guess not."

Shelly cleared a spot on the table. "Is Eric coming? We've only got this room for another twenty minutes."

"He just got on now." Fatima glanced through the glass wall to the cluster of computers in the center of the library. "What is it with old people coming here to look stuff up? My grandparents are online constantly. Skyping with family in Egypt, mostly. That and watching a *ton* of stuff on YouTube. They've got a thing for cat videos."

"Is that where you're from, Egypt?"

"My family, yeah," Fatima said. "Alexandria. They moved here before I was born." Then, after a pause, she said, "You go to St. Anne's."

"I did. They're still deciding if they're going to take me back."

"Are you Catholic?"

"More or less."

"What, you don't believe in it?"

"Parts. The Jesus stuff, yeah, that I believe. It's the other things — the rules on birth control and gays and women priests. That's where the pope and I agree to disagree."

"Do you go to church a lot?"

"Enough," Shelly said, and for a second she thought about adding something on how going to church was better than having to talk to her father's hookups, but it sounded strange in her head, and besides, she knew that wasn't the reason.

Fatima drew circles around random words on the top page. "Is your family really religious?"

"My family isn't really anything."

"Divorced?"

"No, I've never been married."

Fatima laughed. "Duh. I meant your parents."

Shelly smiled and kept it simple. "Yeah, they're divorced. I live with my father."

"Does he make you go to church?"

"He can't make me do anything," Shelly said.

Fatima nodded, and the way she nodded — slow, her head angled down to an empty spot on the table — Shelly could tell there were more questions coming. And that was okay. She had forgotten how good it was to talk. Already it was one of the deepest conversations she had had with a girl her age since the night the police took her away. It felt almost normal. So she waited.

After a minute, Fatima said, "What would happen if you told him you didn't want to go to church anymore?"

Shelly shrugged. "Nothing."

"He wouldn't care?"

"He wouldn't know. And even if he did know, he wouldn't care."

More nodding.

Fatima scooted her chair closer. "Okay, what would happen if you told your parents you didn't believe in it anymore?"

"In what? Going to church?"

"No, not that," Fatima said, her voice just above a whisper, glancing around as she said it. "What if you told them you didn't believe in God?"

Shelly leaned back to think. She knew the answer to the question — they wouldn't care one way or the other — but what she didn't know was why Fatima had asked. She looked across the table at her, at her white hijab and her espresso-dark eyes.

A second later, she had it.

Shelly leaned in and said, "That's your secret."

Fatima's mouth dropped open.

"That's your secret," Shelly said again. "You don't believe in God."

"How did you . . . ?"

"Oh, please, you all but said it."

She reached out and gripped Shelly's hand. "Promise me you won't tell anyone. Not even Eric."

"Don't worry," Shelly said, chuckling as she said it, working her hand free. "I won't tell anybody. But seriously, it's no big deal. A lot of people don't believe in God."

"I didn't say that I don't," Fatima said, sighing, shaking her head, looking down at her hands. "The truth is, I'm not sure what I believe anymore. I'm still trying to figure it out. And I'd appreciate you not laughing at me."

"Sorry," Shelly said. "I just think it's funny that *that's* your horrible secret. Everybody has times when they have doubts. I know I did. I still do."

"Yeah, well, you're not a Muslim."

"I bet some doubters are."

She looked at Shelly. "You have no idea. In Islam it's, like, this major sin to even *question* if God is real. You're not even supposed to *think* about it."

"I'm pretty sure Christianity has something like that too. It's how religions keep you in line."

"But you believe in God, right? You're *sure* God is real."

Shelly nodded. "Yeah, I am."

"See, that's just it. I'm *not* sure. And the more I think about it, the *less* I believe. And I can't *stop* thinking about it either."

"So what? So you don't believe in God. Or you're not sure. Whatever. It's a personal thing between you and God. Or you and nothing."

"Easy for you to say. You said yourself your family doesn't care. *My* family . . ." She let it trail off, and in the silence that followed, Shelly gasped.

"Are you saying your family would . . . would . . . *hurt* you?"

It was Fatima's turn to laugh. "Like an honor killing, that kind of thing? You're watching too much *Dateline.*"

"Sorry," Shelly said again, "but the way you made it sound, it was like, you know . . ."

"Yeah, I know," Fatima said. "And I suppose it *does* happen, so I can't really blame you for thinking that. Plus, you don't know my family. They would never hurt me. Ever."

"So they'd be okay with it?"

"*No way.* It would *kill* them. My parents, my grandparents, my aunts and uncles . . . they would be *devastated.*"

Shelly could relate.

"You have *no idea* how it would hurt them to know that I even had *tiny* doubts. I mean, that's, like, the number-one thing a Muslim parent has to do: raise their kids to be good Muslims. Having one of them turn out an atheist?"

"You don't know that you are."

"The problem," Fatima said, "is that I don't know that I'm not. And that I'm even *thinking* about it."

Shelly looked through the glass wall. Eric was still at the computer. They were running low on time, but they needed his results to solve anything, so there was nothing to do but wait. Then she remembered something she had written on one of the big sheets of paper the day before. She flipped through the pile till she found it. "You said your secret was a book."

"It is. Two books, really. The secret's in one of them."

"Like a diary?"

"No, it's a regular book," Fatima said.

Shelly shrugged. "I don't see a problem with that. I mean, you just had the book. It's not like you wrote it."

"No, but I wrote *in* it. In the margins, on the blank pages . . ."

"Yeah, I noticed you do that a lot," Shelly said, nodding at the papers on the table already crammed with notes.

"And of course I highlighted the best parts."

"That'll make it easy for someone to know what you're thinking."

"It gets even easier. There were a bunch of papers in it too. Sort of letters to myself."

"Like a diary . . ."

"Fine, a diary. All in my handwriting. My parents read those?" She closed her eyes and rubbed her temples. "Thinking about it gives me a headache."

"What you wrote or what you believe?"

"Both."

"What's the other book?"

"It's a little address notebook. I've had it forever," Fatima said, her thumb and forefinger stretched to show the size and shape. "It's got the names and addresses and phone numbers and email addresses for every person I know."

"An address book? Seriously?"

"I know, I know. But I like to write things down, remember?"

It got quiet, and they sat at the table, looking out through the glass wall to the rest of the library, enjoying the semi-soundproof silence. A few minutes later, Eric stood up, and they watched him watching the papers spit out of the printer by the resource desk. Hand on her chin, Fatima said, "You think he's cute?"

"Eh. Okay, I guess."

"That's it? Okay?"

"He's not really my type."

"Hello? Good-looking, kinda jacked, dresses nice?" Fatima laughed. "What's *your* type?"

Shelly grinned. Postapocalyptic razor beat, dark-industrial, techno-goth punk, with brown eyes and black hair and a shy smile. Not that she'd dated someone like that or even met a guy her age who came close, but even with all the shit she was dealing with, the million more important things on her mind, a girl could dream.

And in that dream, she'd bump into this guy somewhere, like a Starbucks or Hot Topic, and he'd have on a Komor Kommando T-shirt or a T3RR0R 3RR0R patch on a leather jacket, and he'd see her old-school Thrill Kill Kult hoodie, and right there they'd have a connection, since how often do you run into somebody who likes those bands in this town? So they'd get a coffee or whatever, and they'd be talking and everything would be so easy and —

"Has he got a girlfriend?"

Shelly shook her head clear. "Who?"

"Eric."

"I think so," Shelly said, imagining the picture she knew was out there. "At least he did."

"Figures," Fatima said. Then she looked at Shelly. "You know something? I'm glad I met you. Well, not *how* we met or *why*, but I'm still glad."

"Thanks," Shelly said. Then, "Me, too."

"My mom's been hyper-restrictive on me lately. She

made me promise not to talk to any of my real friends till I'm back at school."

"Oh."

"But you don't count, since I met you after she told me."

"Wow, lucky me," Shelly said, her tone slipping past Fatima, whose smile didn't change.

"And you know what else? I'm glad you know my secret."

"Hmm."

"It felt like this weight I was carrying everywhere. I couldn't tell my friends, because you know how friends can be."

"Trust me, I know."

"And I'm not stupid enough to talk about it online. Besides, a Muslim saying she has doubts about her faith? No offense, the Christians would be all trying to convert me. And Muslims take everything so frickin' seriously. *Anyway*," she said as Eric came in the door, "I'm just glad I could tell somebody."

He pulled up a chair and sat down. "Tell somebody what?"

"That I've got five minutes before my mother picks me up," Fatima said.

"And we've only got two days to solve this," Shelly said, uncapping a black Sharpie.

TWENTY-ONE

ERIC WAS IN THE PARKING LOT OF THE GYM WHEN HIS grandmother's old phone wailed. He yanked it open, the blue-gray screen sputtering on, and when he saw the number, his heart thumped in his chest. He swallowed hard, forced himself calm, and said hello.

"I hope you don't mind me calling like this," April said.

"No, it's okay," Eric said, no idea what to say, so he said, "Hi."

She gave that little laugh that he'd missed hearing. "Hi."

Now what? Tell her how much he'd been thinking about her, how much she meant to him, how he hated not seeing her, not talking to her, and now not knowing what to say when they did talk? "How you doing?"

"I'm doing good," she said, and there was that laugh again. "I'd ask you the same thing, but . . ."

"Yeah. Well . . ." Well? *Well*? That's it?

"I hear Garrett stopped by to see you."

Now he laughed.

"He didn't do anything stupid, did he?"

"No," Eric said, the lung-busting sprint to catch the last bus as it pulled out of the gas station popping into his head. "He just sorta, you know, did the big-brother talk thing. That's all."

"He can be like that," April said. "He gets it from my parents."

Eric could see it. The friendly intimidation, the all-seeing, all-knowing swagger, the need to be in control, the underlying threat of violence. Like father and mother, like son.

"So, are you, like, suspended forever or expelled or something?"

He said, "Just for the week. I'll be back Monday." But he thought, *Unless that picture gets out.* She was quiet, but he knew what she was thinking, so he told her without waiting to be asked. "I don't know what I was doing. It was stupid and ridiculous. I just . . . I don't know."

He could hear her breathing, could imagine her twirling her hair around her finger like she always did when she was on the phone.

"Basically, I feel like an asshole," he said.

"You should," she said.

"Good. I do." He paused, thought for a second, closed his eyes, and said it. "What happened?"

"You should know, you were there."

"Not that," he said. "Us. What happened?"

April sighed. "Eric . . ."

Eric.

Not *hon,* not *babe.* Eric.

"We went over this."

"I know," he said.

"Things happened so fast."

"Yeah."

"I mean, you had just broken up with Simone, and I was still sorta seeing Nate . . . It just got really intense really fast, that's all. I wasn't ready for it. And neither were you."

Eric felt himself nodding along, all of it true. But that didn't make it easier to hear.

"I need more time," she said. "That probably doesn't make any sense —"

"Yeah, it does," he said, even though no, it didn't.

"Thanks," she said.

Then it got quiet again and he could picture her close, smell the perfume he'd given her on her neck, feel the warmth of her body against his.

I love you.

He wanted to say it, needed to hear it. But he knew it was too soon for that.

"So, *anyway,*" he said, dragging the word out like one

of her crazy-ass girlfriends. "Next week, you see me at school, I'll completely understand if you totally ignore me."

"We'll see," she said, her goodbye lost in her beautiful laugh.

Shelly loved when she timed it right.

Her father's coffee cup was in the sink, but the pot was still warm, and that meant that she had *just* missed him and had the house to herself all night.

Golly, what a *shame*.

She dropped her backpack on a kitchen chair and picked up the note her father had left on the table:

> *Hey,*
> > *Get your homework done early.*
> > *There's some pasta in the fridge if you*
> > *want to heat it up. Or you can order a pizza.*
> > *Don't bother waiting up for me.*
> > *Jeff*

Shelly thought it was an old note she had forgotten to toss out until she noticed a final line.

> *PS — You got a letter.*

They came every couple of weeks, a handwritten address on an orange-trimmed Home Depot envelope, enough pages folded inside to require an extra stamp. Shelly had never read any of them, but she could guess what they said.

They probably started off with a time-based reminder that would pick away at the scab — *7 months, 3 weeks, 5 days, 12 hours, and 25 minutes ago* — then maybe cut to some sort of mental picture — *how happy he was, how he loved to smile* — then a reality check or two — *the call from the hospital* or *what it was like to turn down the street and see all the police cars* — for sure several paragraphs of insults, curses, and threats, wrapping the whole thing up with a wish-you-were-never-born finale.

And there it was, propped up against the plastic flower centerpiece.

She picked up the envelope. Three, maybe four pages inside, the paper crinkly from her mother's firm hand-writing.

Shelly knew there was a chance that the letter wasn't anything like what she'd imagined, a chance that it wasn't fueled by hate and intentionally cruel. There was even a chance that it might hint at some far-off forgiving, some come-home invitation.

There was a chance, all right.

Same as a snowball's in hell.

She left her father's note on the table and dropped the unopened envelope in the garbage.

TWENTY-TWO

THE FIRST THING HIS MOTHER SAID WHEN SHE GOT HOME from work was "How was your day?"

Considering the shit that was going to be hitting the fan soon, it was a good day, and Eric told her so. Conversation over, she announced that they were having hamburgers for dinner and asked him to get a fire started so the grill would be ready when his dad got home.

Burgers *and* the chance to play with fire? She didn't have to ask twice.

Twenty minutes later — after half a quart of lighter fluid and roof-high flames — the coals settled down to a glow and Eric sat on the steps of the deck with his iPad and checked for Facebook updates.

Apparently something "absolutely frickin LMFAO hysterical!" had happened Saturday night at an undisclosed location involving shaving cream, vodka, a math textbook, and a page ripped from *Playboy,* and this event then led to a lot of repostings of lyrics from old Gorillaz songs and references to somebody named Sir Jasper of the Dip. Oh, and Marshall and Rosi were now officially a couple. Whoever they were.

Outta the loop for a few days, and it might as well have been forever.

There was a picture from a party at some senior's house, and there in the background, almost invisible, was Ian, the guy who'd filmed his now-infamous mac and cheese attack and posted it on YouTube.

He and Ian weren't friends because Ian didn't have friends. And he seemed to like it that way, roaming the halls of the school with his black band T-shirts and black skinny jeans, black vests in the fall, black trench coat in the winter, his straight black hair keeping one eye always hidden. Too big to get picked on, and weird enough to pull a knife on the fool who'd try. There were plenty of rumors about him, and if only half were true, he was a guy you didn't want to mess with. But it was those rumors that had had Eric tracking him down after school, and he didn't flinch when Eric described it, no what-if-I-get-in-trouble? or what-will-the-coach-say? Just a simple cash transaction and it was done.

True, Eric hadn't paid him yet, but he assumed that Ian would understand and there'd be time to make good on it.

Besides, there wasn't much Ian could do about it now anyway.

There was a friend request from Fatima, and he clicked on confirm.

She was cool and, from what he could see, good-looking.

Her headscarf covered her hair and ears, and she wore it tight under her chin, framing her face in white cloth. She had gorgeous dark eyes, and her skin had this tint to it, something between tan and brown, what April would have called an olive complexion. She had a great smile, too, which didn't hurt. But it was probably a conversation with some guy that was behind her big secret, and the last thing he needed was another older brother threatening to kick his ass.

It was Fatima's idea that she take home all the stuff they had printed out about their victims to see if she could find anything in common. She seemed excited by the challenge and promised a full report, and both he and Shelly were happy to let her do it. But even if she found something, they were running out of time to do anything. It was already Tuesday night. Thursday at this time, it'd be too late.

Wait, *when* on Thursday?

What was the deadline?

Noon?

After school?

Midnight?

First thing in the morning?

He wondered if it was in one of the caller's old messages, so he clicked on Gmail, rekeying his password and hitting ENTER.

That's when he saw the subject line for the new message.

Check out the hot picture I took of April!

For a lifetime he didn't move, didn't breathe, then a finger shot out and tapped open the email.

And there it was again.

The picture that started it all.

Taken with a camera app on an iPhone from the foot of the bed.

His bed. In his room.

Hi-res and in perfect focus.

Her head on the pillow, hands gripping the ends, eyes closed, a half smile biting closed on her lower lip, her blond hair all over the place, the earrings her parents had given her earlier that day for her seventeenth birthday catching the light from the flash.

The rumpled sheets made her early-summer tan look golden dark, and where she wasn't tan, her skin glowed pinkish white. The bellybutton ring her mother said she was too young to have impossible to miss in the center of the photo.

Next to the bed, in a pile on the desk, her teal Abercrombie T-shirt, white Victoria's Secret bra, and black Wet Seal thong.

The way the camera had been held—high overhead, stretched up, trying to capture it all, a crazy-angle lucky shot—the photo showed another leg—lean, muscular, an unmistakable J-shaped scar from an ancient bike accident, still visible above his knee.

She had said, "Don't even think of taking any pictures."

And when the flash went off, she said, "Delete it now."

Later she said, "Swear you deleted it."

Swear it.

That was three months ago.

Eight weeks later, it was over, the picture the only reminder of what used to be.

A picture he said he wouldn't take.

A picture he swore he'd delete.

A picture a stranger now had.

There was more.

Above the picture—separated by semicolons in tiny, eight-point type—the names, numbers, and email addresses of every contact on his phone.

The iPad bounced as his knees started to shake. He stood up fast, and the dizziness brought him right back down. He forced in a gulp of air and felt his stomach lurch, the roaring sound in his head making it hard to think, the voice in his head—his voice—screaming that it was already too late.

He got up, slower this time, and walked away from the house, toward the pine trees that lined the edge of the yard.

That picture.

No doubt at all as to who it was.

Where it was taken.

Or who had held the camera.

And now everybody he knew would have their own, personal copy.

Instinct made him scroll down past the picture, and that's where he found the note.

Thought you'd like to see the message I'll be sending out Thursday! ;P

The fifth time he read the line, he got it.

He was still safe.

His knees went wobbly again, so he sat down on the grass. He thought for a moment, then his fingers raced across the screen, adding the phantom email address to his contact list, trashing the email, then opening the deleted-items folder and erasing it from there. He knew that you could never totally delete anything, and that the picture was still buried somewhere in the megabytes, but this way it would be hard to stumble on, say, if a parent accidentally on purpose went snooping.

He still had time before his father got home, so he opened a blank email and pasted in the address. In the subject line, he typed, *Thursday*.

Got the message. I'll be making the delivery you asked for, but then that's it. I'll need extra time on Thursday to get the

video posted. It should be up by Saturday morning at the latest.

Eric hit SEND, and before he had time to close out, he had a response.

Thursday by 9:00 p.m. At 9:01 the picture gets sent. :(

The caller had been waiting.

The more he thought about it, the madder he got, the more he knew he'd find a way to get even. Now he waited, somehow knowing there was more.

Soon enough, another email binged in, and when he tapped it open, squared-off digital numbers of a count-down clock filled the screen.

49:26:59

49 hours.

26 minutes.

59 seconds.

Ticking down to nothing.

49:26:58

49:26:57

49:26:56

49:26:55

49:26:54

49:26:53

49:26:52

49:26:51

Fatima watched the numbers change.

It was hypnotic.

Relaxing, even.

The seconds were marked with a baby-bird peep, and the minutes with a water drop. She wondered what the changing hours sounded like. Probably another nature sound — an owl hoot or a cricket, maybe. She was sure that the final alarm would be a crack of thunder with a flash of hot lightning, since that was pretty much how she saw her family reacting to the scanned pages the caller would be emailing out.

The reproduction quality was amazing, at least 300 dpi. You could clearly see the curlicues at the ends of the *Y*'s, the little half circles that dotted the *I*'s and made her handwriting so distinct. And you could read every word, even the ones scrunched between lines of text, the dense paragraphs of declarative sentences that clarified the depth of her doubt. All without magnification. Even Teyta Noor, with her thick glasses and old-woman squint, could read it. And she would, too. Every damning word.

Fatima had thought she'd die right there when she opened the email and saw those addresses and those scans of the pages. And when she realized it was just a warning, that the email had only been sent to her, she sighed so loud that she startled herself, giggling with relief.

That all changed with the counter, and the realization of what would happen when it hit zero.

It even took the thrill out of solving the mystery.

Okay, maybe it wasn't *solved,* but she was sure that it was cracked.

What had looked impossible turned out to be easy, a simple task of compilation, organization, elimination, and analysis. The same process that got her in this trouble in the first place.

When Fatima combined the pile of papers she had printed out about Connor Stark with the ones Shelly had found on Katie Schepler and the ones Eric had on Heather Herman, the stack was three inches thick. Scores of pages and hundreds of posts, with twice as many names and places and events to sort through, plus links and Foursquare check-ins and lists of friends and profile info and lines and lines and lines of Tweets. Eric had said it couldn't be done, so of course she knew she had to do it. The cuter the guy, the more competitive she got, a stupid, uncontrollable urge that explained why she couldn't get a boyfriend.

At least, she hoped it was the explanation.

She had started by spreading the papers out on her bed, the floor, the dresser, the chair. She assigned highlighters —yellow for school, pink for sports, blue for religion, purple for community service, lime green for everything else —then started in with the stack on her desk.

The first pages took the longest, but then she found her

rhythm, her left brain sifting, compiling, subcategorizing, and cross-referencing, her right brain forming hypotheses, pulling patterns out of reams of random data, zoning out the distractions, zeroing in on the answers. Then logic took over, analyzing everything, dismissing the unproven, following the evidence, knowing that the truth would be waiting at the end.

And two hours later, there it was, the one thing all three of their victims had in common, the single element within the subset of C union K union H.

She still had to check her work, start from scratch and do the whole thing over again to be sure, looking for holes in her thinking, simple slip-ups that would give a false positive. Still, the first run-through was looking good.

If Shelly was right, it would tell them who the caller was. And if they knew who the caller was, they could keep their secrets from getting out.

That was the idea, anyway.

Now, would it work?

Probably not, but she still smiled. She had solved the puzzle — at least one part of it — and she'd done it in half the time she'd thought it would take.

It's what she did best.

The gift that made science and math so easy.

The curse that made faith so hard.

Then there were all those *What ifs* that drove her nuts.

What if she had walked down a different row in the library?

She wouldn't have seen the book.

What if her eyes were scanning the shelf above or the shelf below?

She would never have noticed the title.

What if she hadn't slowed down, tilting her head sideways to read?

It would just have been a yellow blur, another cover on another book she'd walked past.

But she had gone down that aisle, looked at that row, and read that title.

God Is Not Great.

The second she read it, her gift took over, analyzing the words without being asked, the hypothesis involuntarily tested against previous truths.

Allah Akbar.

God is great.

The truth she had always accepted.

The only truth she had ever known.

The truth that gave her life meaning.

That held the universe together.

It must be true.

It *had* to be true.

Because if not . . .

At first she tried going back, pretending she hadn't

seen it, shrugging it off as some stupid rant by an ignorant fool. She had heard things like that lots of times before, things about Islam being violent or how it said it was okay to abuse women. But she knew they were wrong. She had the proof, chapter and verse, right there in her Quran. Yet somehow this one title had gotten past that line of defense, snuck into her brain, and wouldn't go away, a horrible song that played over and over.

God Is Not Great.

It had to be wrong.

It said so in the Quran.

Besides, *everybody* knew it was wrong. Christians, Jews, Hindus . . . everybody.

That should've been good enough.

But it wasn't.

Her gift wouldn't let her off that easy, digging into the logic problem like it was bonus points on a physics exam.

Two days later, she was back, *accidentally* walking down the same aisle, *randomly* picking the book up off the shelf, *sorta* reading for a little while, the little while becoming a longer while, then a day later, checking the book out, taking it to school, hiding the laminate cover under a paper dust jacket from a biography of Lincoln, renewing it twice before being told she'd reached the renewal limit, warned yet again about writing in the margins. Finally, at the mall bookstore, a paperback copy of the book sandwiched between an issue of *People* and the CliffsNotes to *The Great Gatsby*. She had an it's-for-a-friend line ready, but the clerk simply rang it up and put it in the bag, no questions asked.

At least someone had no questions.

Even then, she still could have explained it all away, why she had a copy of such an evil book. But her gift, her curse, forced her hand, highlighting passages, scribbling in the margins, filling the end pages with notes, adding Islam-based examples the author had overlooked.

She couldn't help herself. She'd had to know.

And now that she knew, no one could help her.

Alone, she tapped a pencil on her desk in time with the seconds on the screen.

49:26:50
49:26:49
49:26:48
49:26:47

49:26:46
49:26:45
49:26:44
49:26:43
49:26:42

With a few clicks of her mouse, Shelly changed the screen saver on her computer, replacing the image from Aesthetic Perfection's "The Great Depression" video with the countdown clock. The red numbers popped on the black background, giving her whole room a fiery glow.

She hadn't noticed when the message with the clock had popped in, too busy staring at the subject line of the first email.

Marceli Romano.

There wasn't anything else in that first email.

There didn't have to be.

Her new look, the cross-state move, Jeff's last name? None of it had worked.

The caller knew who she was.

And if the caller knew that, then the caller knew what she had done.

It had been kept out of the news—her name, the details, all of it—but obviously that didn't matter. Maybe she had seen the police report or talked to somebody at the hospital or her old school. Or the morgue.

Whatever.

The caller knew, and that's all that mattered.

There was a time when it seemed everybody knew. That's when friends had stopped being friends, everyone else whispering behind her back, her mother crying every time she saw her. Even Father Tony seemed to change, the Cain and Abel story coincidentally coming up Sunday after Sunday, the message of every sermon circling back to the "challenge of forgiveness."

The real challenge had been at home. She had to give them credit — they made it through the spring and most of the summer before shipping her off to a near stranger who, by law, had to take her in.

For the people behind the dozens of email addresses pasted below the countdown clock, it would all come as a horrible shock.

Starting in 49 hours, 26 minutes, and 42 seconds.

Shelly recognized a few of the names on the list, girls at St. Anne's who she hung with, girls she liked and who seemed to like her, the ones who were as close to friends as she thought she'd ever have again.

But they were human and wouldn't be able to resist the urge.

Then they'd start asking questions. Not of her, of course. Other than forced hellos, they wouldn't talk to her at all. There'd be that one who, on a dare, would sit with her at lunch or ask to borrow a pen, but that would be all any of them would say to her, so they'd have to come up with their own answers to questions —

Why'd she do it?

Is she crazy?

Shouldn't she be in jail?

The funny thing is, if they did ask, she would tell them.

I don't know.

Probably.

Yes.

But she still had time.

Two days to keep Shelly Meyer from turning back into Marceli Romano.

In the red-hued darkness, she watched her time tick away.

49:26:41
49:26:40
49:26:39
49:26:38
49:26:37

TWENTY-THREE

"THAT'S IT?"

"That's it."

"Are you sure?"

"Positive."

"And that's the *only* thing?"

"No. But it's the only thing that matters."

Eric and Shelly looked at each other, then back up at Fatima, holding the fifth and final sheet of her presentation.

The first three sheets, taped on the glass wall by the door, had the names of their victims written across the top in black marker. Below each name were color-coded lists — mined from Facebook and Twitter and other must-be-on sites — of the things, events, people, and places in their lives. Yellow for school, pink for sports, blue for religion, purple for community service, lime green for everything else.

The fourth sheet, tacked to the bulletin board, was a mess of words and names and arrows, with things circled and highlighted and underlined and crossed out and written over.

On the last sheet, in capital letters three inches tall:
THE CUBIT SUMMER THEATER PROGRAM.

"They have some friends in common too," Fatima said, nodding at a yellow legal pad on the table, "but I checked a bunch of them, and they were all in that program."

Shelly spun the pad around and ran her finger down the names. "So there could still be something else, some person you didn't check."

"There could be. But this is it."

"It makes sense," Eric said. "My guy? Connor? He's a big theater geek."

"They all are," Fatima said. "That's what they have in common. Look at the charts."

"Wait a sec. There *is* no theater at St. Anne's. I ought to know, I go there."

"That may be true. But Heather still *does* theater." Fatima dropped the sheet onto the table and stepped to the posters. "In eighth grade, she was in the chorus in the West Bloomfield Congregational Church production of *Godspell,* she played Bunny Byron in *Babes in Arms* at some workshop thingy two summers ago, she was in a musical revue at Limelight Dance Studio. Aaaannnd . . ." Fatima leaned over to the bulletin board and tapped a green box on the fourth sheet. "Two months ago, she was Hedy La Rue in the Cubit Summer Theater production of *How to Succeed in Business Without Really Trying.*"

"What about Connor?"

"He was there. He played somebody called Bud Frump," Fatima said, squinting to read her tiny writing. "And my girl Katie had the female lead in the show. Rosemary Pilkington. She got to kiss J. Pierrepont Finch."

Eric shrugged. "Who's that?"

"I don't know," Fatima said, "but he was played by this cute guy with gorgeous blue eyes."

"I've got blue eyes," Eric said.

Fatima grinned. "Anyway, from what I pieced together, this is where they met. The Cubit Summer Theater Program."

Shelly looked at the posters, at the notes on the table, then up at Fatima, a smile slowly spreading. "Oh my god. I don't believe it. You did it. You *really did* it."

Eric said, "Hold on, wasn't this compare-and-contrast thing *your* idea?"

"Yeah. But I didn't think it was actually going to work."

"So all that research the other day—that could have all been a waste of time?"

"Could have. Turns out it wasn't. Thanks to Fatima."

"I told you, I love this stuff," Fatima said, waving a hand at the posters as she sat down, leaning across the table to bump fists with Shelly.

"Okay, great. We have the connection," Eric said. "All

three of them were in the same summer theater program, they were all in the same play —"

"Actually, it's a musical."

"Whatever. The point is, what do we do now?"

Shelly started to say something, stopped, then leaned back slowly in her chair, her eyes losing focus as she thought. Next to her, Fatima began filling her paper with scribbled lines and connecting arrows. Eric stared up at the fluorescent lights of the study room.

For five minutes, no one said anything, the scratching of Fatima's pencil sounding loud in the small room.

Then Shelly said, "Something bad happened at that theater camp."

Eric laughed. "Sounds like a line from a slasher movie."

"No, seriously, think about it," Shelly said. "Our caller wants us to go after three specific people who were at that camp. So something bad had to happen there to make her go through all this."

"Go through what? We're the ones doing the work."

"True," Shelly said. "But she had to find a way to get us to do it for her. That couldn't have been easy."

Eric nodded. "Sounds like payback. And how much you wanna bet it had something to do with a plate of macaroni and cheese?"

Shelly flipped the poster board over and started writing. "Let's assume Heather, Connor, and Katie did the same things to our caller that she's making us do to them."

"Makes sense," Eric said. "That would explain why we all got the same instructions. Bump 'em in the hallways, call 'em names —"

"Make them cry," Shelly said.

"— all leading up to the mac-and-cheese finale."

Fatima scribbled notes in the corner of the poster. "So what we need to do is find out *who* they picked on and we'll have our caller."

"It's that simple."

"What, we just *ask* them?"

"In a way, yeah," Shelly said.

"I'm not talking to Katie," Fatima said. "She scares me."

"And Connor's too scared of me to say a word," Eric said.

"You don't have to. We do what we did when we looked at their Facebook pages. I'll talk to Katie, you talk to Heather, and Fatima will talk to Connor."

"It doesn't matter who gets who," Eric said. "They're not going to talk to us."

"Oh yes they will," Shelly said. "They're going to tell you everything we need to know, and they're going to love doing it."

"Sure they will."

"And they'll fill in all the details we don't know, too. You'll see."

Eric laughed. "You're crazy."

"This whole thing is crazy," Fatima said. "The people we bullied bullied the girl who's bullying us."

"So in the end, we're all victims," Eric said.

"Yeah," Shelly said. "And we're all bullies."

TWENTY-FOUR

HIS PHONE RANG AT 7:00 P.M. SHARP.

Shelly was right.

"Send them a message on Facebook," she had said as they took down the posters in the study room. "Tell them you're the teen reporter for some local arts magazine and you're working on a story about young actors. Say, 'I contacted the Cubit Theater Program and they gave me your name.' Tell them you've got a tight deadline, give them your phone number, ask them to call you tonight at seven. They'll be watching the clock, waiting to call."

Eric flipped open the brick-size phone. "Hello?"

"Hi, Eric, this is Heather Herman? You sent me a Facebook message asking me to call you? About an interview for the paper or something?"

He said hello, thanked her for calling, then rattled off the story that he, Shelly, and Fatima had come up with at the library. He knew it was going to be easy when Heather went on about how much she loved the articles in *Scene It*, Fatima's imaginary magazine. He started down the checklist of the warm-up questions — what drew you to the stage, how long have you been acting, what was your first part ever, how do you prepare for a role—half listening to her answers as he sliced floating fruit on his iPad. After fifteen minutes, she took a breath, and Eric steered the conversation where it needed to go.

"I talked to this guy at the Cubit Theater Program—Aaron or Trevor or . . ."

"Stephen?"

Right again. "Yeah, that's it. Stephen. He said that you were one of the best students he had this summer—"

"Oh, I don't know if I was *that* good . . ."

"That's what he said. And he said there were three of you that showed real potential and that I should ask you what it was like working with, uh, Bud Frump and . . ." Eric paused a beat, as if checking his notes. "Rosemary Plinker?"

"Rosemary Pilkington," Heather said, laughing. "Those are two characters in the musical we did. *How to Succeed in Business Without Really Trying.* Do you know it?"

"I thought it was a class you took," he said, kicking it up into flirt mode. "You were Hedy La Rue, right?"

"Yeah, it was a cool part because I had—"

He steered her back. "So, who were the other actors?"

"Connor Stark played Bud—he was *so* funny. There was one point—"

"And who played Rosemary?"

"Katie Schepler. It's the lead role. She's really pretty."

"Funny, that's what Stephen said about you," Eric said, voice dropping a bit, laying it on thick.

"He *did?* That's sorta creepy. He's, like, my father's age."

"He didn't mean it that way," Eric said, backpedaling. "It was more like you were perfect for the role."

"But Hedy's kinda slutty . . ."

Great. Stick to the script. "Tell me what it was like, you, Connor, and Katie, all in the same show."

Fatima glanced at the alarm clock by the side of her bed. 7:34.

Over twenty minutes and Connor Stark was still on the same question. At this rate it would be after midnight before he got around to anything important.

She'd followed the script, just like they wrote it out, and he gave her the answers that Shelly said he'd give, more or less. She'd gotten up to the part about the other two, Heather and Katie, and that's where it was stuck. First he had that long, dull story about how they met at orientation, which at some point morphed into an even duller story about how they struggled to get those roles, how they each approached their characters differently, but how, when the curtain went up opening night, they just, well, *jelled.* Whatever that meant.

Connor was trying way too hard to imply that he and Katie had, you know, fooled around, but he wasn't that good of an actor, the whole thing sounding like a script he recited to reassure himself he was straight. It was more boring than sad. When she heard him say something about his muse, she knew she had to act fast.

"You guys ever do any crazy stuff?"

"*All* actors are a bit crazy. That's acting, isn't it? As Oscar Wilde once said—"

"I mean offstage. When you were just hanging out. You had to do *something* to stay loose. Did you guys ever do anything kinda crazy?"

Connor chuckled in that stupid *playa* way. "Well, one time—and I can't believe I'm telling you this—Katie and I—"

"I meant like practical jokes," Fatima said. "*That* kind of stuff."

Again with the laugh. "Oh, the stories I could tell you."

Fatima put a giggle in her voice. "*Excellent.* Tell me one. And you can skip the hand-in-warm-water kind of thing. I want the *good* stuff."

So he told her about hiding a condom in a chorus girl's script, swapping out the backing soundtrack to the show with a Wiz Khalifa CD, having twenty pizzas delivered to the cafeteria at dinnertime, truth-or-dare setups, and way too many toilet-paper pranks. Fatima laughed where it was expected and played shocked when she thought it would lead him on, but then the stories slowed and she could tell he was waiting for another fluffy-light question, something involving his craft or his Broadway dreams. Instead, she went for the kill.

"You're not big on playing by the rules, are you?"

"Gotta do whatcha gotta do," he said, the accent as ghetto as J.Crew.

"Everybody at my school is so freakin' *serious* all the time. Nobody ever does *anything* that could get them in trouble."

"Hey, no risk, no fun, right?"

"Well, I heard you had a *lot* of fun at that theater thing."

He mumbled something, but before he could change the subject, she said, "Like that macaroni-and-cheese video."

For a long moment there was nothing. In the silence, Fatima knew she had gone too far, given away too much.

Then Connor laughed.

"Cut the crap. What's this really about?"

"I told you. I'm doing a story for *Scene It* magazine and —"

"Bullshit. There's no such thing," Katie Schepler said in a flat, matter-of-fact, coplike voice. "And even if there was, they wouldn't waste their time on a story about a bunch of gleeks in a third-rate summer workshop. Right?"

Shelly paused, took a deep breath. "Right."

"Good, that's out of the way. What's your name?"

"I told you. Shelly Meyer."

"Why all the bullshit, Shelly?"

"I'm trying to find out something."

"Obviously."

"Not about you. About the girl you . . . the girl who . . ."

"Come on, out with it. I don't have all night."

"The one you dumped the food on."

"Hmm. Interesting," Katie said. "Why do you want to know?"

"It's kinda complicated."

"No shit, Shelly. That's why you had to make up that stupid magazine story. You a friend of hers or something?"

Shelly laughed. "No. I don't even know her name. She's sort of harassing me and I want to make her stop."

"And you think that knowing her name and what happened at that waste-of-time camp is gonna help?"

"Yeah. I mean, I hope it does."

"What do you know already?"

"Just that you and the other two, Heather and Connor . . . well, one of you dumped a plate of macaroni and cheese on her head, and then somebody posted a video of it."

"Connor did the plate, Heather taped it. I'm the one who put it online."

"Oh," Shelly said, surprised by the ease of the confession.

"What else do you think you know?"

"I'm not sure —"

"Guess."

Shelly shrugged as she switched the phone to her other ear. "The three of you probably picked on this girl. Calling her names, that sort of stuff?"

"Basically you're saying we bullied her."

"Yeah. I guess."

It was quiet for a moment, then a long, exhausted sigh that ended in a whispered string of swear words. Shelly waited, watching the red seconds on the countdown clock tick by.

"The little bitch had it coming."

"Huh?"

"She deserved it. Actually, she got off easy," Katie said. "After what she did to *us*? Yeah, we should have done something worse."

"But I thought —"

"No, you didn't. You didn't think at all. You assumed. A whiny eighth-grade girl gets humiliated by three high school students and right away you know *exactly* what happened. But you haven't got a clue."

"Okay, you're right. I don't know. So tell me."

Katie laughed. "Why the hell should I?"

"Because —" Shelly started to say, then stopped, stumped by the question.

Why *should* this girl help?

Because she got a Facebook message to call a stranger who lied to her to learn about her past?

Because keeping her secrets isn't as important as making sure some stranger's secrets don't get out?

Because the counter was down to 26 hours, 9 minutes and 12 seconds?

"No answer, huh?" Katie laughed again. "Didn't think so. Well, good luck with your—"

"Because if I don't stop her," Shelly said, the words rushing out, "she's going to tell everyone. This *thing* she knows. About me."

"Ooh, secrets," Katie said. "Do tell."

"Look, all I need is her name—"

"Fine," Katie said. "Just tell me your secret."

Shelly ran a hand through her hair, grabbing hold. *"Why?"*

"If I'm going to give you what you want, I should at least get a good story out of it."

"Please. I don't want anyone to know. I mean, things are finally starting to—"

"Oh, I won't tell," Katie said. "I just want to know for me."

"But—"

Katie laughed. "The more you squirm, the more I gotta know."

"She, uh, she knows that I, uh —"

"Shelly? If I think you're lying, you'll never get the name."

Shelly held her hand over her mouth, muffling the sobs.

"So what's it gonna be? Your secret for her name, or no?"

"I . . . I can't . . . please . . ."

"Fine, Shelly. You got my number, call me if you change your —"

"I killed my brother."

Silence.

Then, in a low, curious voice, "Whoa."

"I was babysitting. I did something, and he died."

"That's a serious secret. Do the police —"

"Yes," Shelly said. "They know. After I did it, I called 911. The ambulance arrived, and he was dead, and the police took me away."

Another pause. "Was this, like, recently?"

Yesterday. It was always yesterday. But she said, "This year. February fourteenth."

"Oh. Valentine's Day. That's gotta suck."

Shelly listened to her own breathing on the phone. Short, choppy, uneven, then a sniff, a hard swallow. She could taste the salt on her lips.

After a long minute, Katie said, "Look. Shelly." She

sighed. "Here's what happened, okay? It was the last week at camp. We'd already done the final performance, so mostly it was just hanging out, which was cool, but you know how it is. You've been together that long, there's just some faces you're sick of seeing. There's no rule that says you have to be friends with everybody, right? Well, one night it was Connor's birthday, and Heather finds out he's never gotten high. I mean, the guy's turning *fifteen* and he's never even *seen* a joint. Can you imagine?"

Shelly could imagine.

"So we buy a fat spliff off one of the landscape guys and we take a walk. Just the three of us, on this trail a half mile away from the dorms. We fire it up and hilarity ensues. The next day, the three of us are hauled into the counselor's office. Seems we weren't as alone as we thought. Oh, and of course she didn't turn us in to get us in trouble. *Noooo*, it was because she *cared* about us and didn't want us to do anything quote-unquote stupid. She was just mad we didn't invite her along."

"Did you get in trouble?"

"*Pffft*. They knew that if they blew us in, *they'd* be the ones in deep shit. My parents would have gone *ballistic* on them. My mom's an attorney, so she'd be all for suing their asses. In the end, we weren't allowed to go to the big pizza-party bonfire on Saturday night — whoop-de-do, right? Plus, we had to work extra kitchen duty. You know, scraping plates and loading the dishwasher. Scrubbing the big pots. That's when we saw her in the cafeteria. I quick slopped some cold mac and cheese on a paper plate, and Connor ran out and dumped it on her. Heather filmed it on her phone."

"Didn't anybody try to stop you?"

"Nobody saw us."

"Wait. I thought it was in the middle of lunch."

"What, you think we're stupid? The cafeteria was empty, she was just cutting through. We all laughed — well, not her — then she ran off and took a shower. I don't think she ever told anyone. At least, I never heard about it again."

"But people saw it when you put it online."

"Saw what? It was shot on an old phone from way across a dark cafeteria. You can't see shit. And I just had it up a couple of days. I think the only people who saw it were us. It was stupid."

Shelly thought about the caller's instructions, how it had to be at school, in the cafeteria, close to noon and everybody watching, and remembered something Jeff once said about payback being a bitch.

"Anyway, that's what happened. I haven't kept in touch with Heather or Connor. Facebook friends, but that's about it. And not even on my real list. It was one of those camp things. You're friends there, but back in the real world, you've got nothing in common."

Like a Catholic baby killer, a jock pornographer, and an atheist Muslim.

"So promise me something," Katie said. "This little shit? You teach her a lesson."

Shelly took a breath. "That's the plan."

TWENTY-FIVE

A FEW MINUTES AFTER EIGHT, HIS GRANDMOTHER'S OLD phone started ringing. He was in the living room, watching TV, and the phone was upstairs on his bed, but it was loud enough that he could have been down the street and heard it.

The scratched-up screen made it hard to read the incoming number, but he had a good idea who it would be.

"So, I called him," Fatima said.

"And?"

"Everything was going good till I asked him about the macaroni-and-cheese thing."

"What, he freak or something?"

"No, he was just all 'That's ancient history' and 'I've asked God's forgiveness.' I couldn't get anything out of him. How about you? Any luck?"

"She said she heard about it, but claimed she wasn't part of it."

"Think she's telling the truth?"

"I don't know. Maybe. She didn't seem the type."

"Did I seem like the type?"

He smiled. "Have you heard from Shelly?"

"Her phone's busy. I bet she's still talking to Katie. That girl scares me."

"Which one?"

"Both," she said, and laughed. "Katie's pretty, but she's got this look about her, like she'd rip your head off if you made her mad. Shelly's more the sneaky type. She'd find a way to get even."

"Good thing she's on our side."

"What do you think she did?"

"She probably stuck to the script, asked her the questions we came up with. I hope she did better than us, though."

"Not that," Fatima said. "You know. *Her secret.* What do you think she did that was so bad?"

He blinked, and there was Shelly, leaning out of the bus, glaring at him, his joke about her killing someone still hanging in the air. He shook his head and it was gone. "No clue."

"I bet she's pregnant."

"No, she's a virgin," he said, regretting it as he said it.

"And you know that how?"

"It just sorta came up. Something she said. Besides, who'd want to admit to that?"

"There's nothing wrong with being a virgin," Fatima said, her tone shifting. "I'd rather be a virgin than some skank who sleeps with every guy she meets."

"Oh, please. Just because a girl isn't a virgin, that doesn't make her a slut."

"Easy for you to say. You don't know how girls talk. They find out you're nasty? They rip into you. Girls are mean. And all it takes is one asshole guy for a girl to get a slutty reputation."

Eric felt his stomach roll. "Not all guys are like that."

"You're a guy," Fatima said. "Of course you'd say that. This one kid at my school? He took a *video* of his girlfriend in the shower."

"Did you actually see it?"

"Duh, *everybody* saw it."

He switched the phone to his other ear. "What happened to him?"

"Him? Nothing. She moved away, though. *Anyway*," Fatima said, saying it in a way that let him know the subject was closed. "Do you think Shelly will find out who's been calling us?"

"Maybe. She's smart. She figured out that it was a girl. And she's great at getting people to do what they don't want to do. Look at us. Meeting every day, making phone calls."

"I'm just glad she did. I wouldn't have known what to do. There's no way I would have done it on my own."

"You're the one who figured out the link between the victims."

"Yeah, but she told me where to look. That was the hard part."

"I'm still impressed."

"So, tell me the truth," Fatima said. "You think we'll be able to find out who the caller is and stop her?"

He didn't say anything.

"I think there's a good chance we can do it," she said.

God, he hoped so.

The chance they had was slim at best, but he was holding on to it anyway. That and second chances, the kind he prayed he'd be given if the photo started popping up in everyone's inbox. And then there was the chance he tried not to think about at all, the chance that the photo crossed more than just a moral line, the chance that he'd end up on some list of offenders, some national registry, a court-ordered bumper sticker on his car, a sign in front of his house.

"If Shelly gets the girl's name," Fatima said, bringing him back in the moment, "we can, I don't know, do something."

"Like ask her not to do it?"

"We could start with that. Then, if it doesn't work, you could, like, you know, scare her."

"Me? I'm not gonna beat up some girl."

"*Noooo,* you just have to make her *think* you would."

"Well, I wouldn't. So you better have another plan."

"I bet we can probably talk her out of it," Fatima said. "You said yourself that Shelly was good at getting people to do stuff. Why can't she talk this girl out of sending the emails?"

Because the girl is crazy. Because she went this far to get revenge and isn't going to stop because they ask politely. They had to play her game, and that meant no mercy.

"We'll see," he said, thinking.

"It's funny," Fatima said. "I'm not scared of what's going to happen to *me*. I'll get grounded and stuff like that, but that's not what I'm afraid of. I'm afraid of what it's going to do to my parents."

"Yeah, that," he said, an image of his parents staring open-mouthed at the picture on a police-station laptop forcing its way into his head.

"And I know what they're going to say, too."

"Let me guess. 'We're not mad, we're disappointed.'"

"Ugh, I hate that. Plus, they're still mad, no matter what they say."

Eric nodded, smiling at the truth of it all.

"What's funny," Fatima said, "is that my family is going to find out someday anyway."

"Why? Somebody else know?"

"No, I'll end up telling them. I'd have to. I couldn't lie

to them forever. They'll still be hurt, and they're never going to understand, but they'll deal with it. Because they're family." She sighed. "But that's *years* from now. Decades."

"Well, if by some miracle we dodge this bullet, I plan on lying to everyone, forever. At least about this."

"Is it that bad?"

"Oh, yeah."

"Wanna talk about it?"

He laughed. "I don't even want to *think* about it."

TWENTY-SIX

SHE KNEW IT WAS A DREAM.

It was dark, of course, and raining, and there she was, running away from something she couldn't see but that was getting closer. And as she watched herself run — in slow motion, and clumsy — Shelly could hear herself saying, "Running in a dream? How cliché." The sound of her own voice startled her awake, and when she sat up, it took a moment for her to place where she was and how long she'd been there.

"Rise and shine like the sun, Miss Shelly," Father Joe shouted from across the empty church, the Thursday-morning crowd of twelve already gone.

Shelly rubbed her eyes as the priest made his way down the aisle. "How long have I been asleep?"

"I saw you start to nod off during my sermon. You were not alone. Mrs. Mitchell, also. But she falls asleep several times during every mass."

"Sorry," Shelly said as she yawned. "I haven't been sleeping good at night, and it's so warm in here this morning."

"Then I am truly glad that my words were able to help

you." He sat at the end of the row, draping a long arm over the back of the pew. "The church is here to provide comfort, and sometimes that means a place to sleep."

Shelly massaged her shoulder. "If they're serious about comfort, you might want to pad these seats."

Father Joe thought a moment, then laughed. "I see what you are doing. You are using the different meanings of the words *comfort* and *comfortable* to make a joke. Very clever, miss."

She stretched and yawned again.

"What is it that is keeping you from getting a good night's sleep?"

"Nothing," she said. "Just a little problem I have to solve."

"A school problem? Perhaps I can help. I was top of my class in maths."

"Not that kind of problem. Something personal," she said. Then, sensing he'd still want to help, she added, "It's a female thing."

"Ah, well then," the priest said, backing away from his offer. "I pray it will all work out for the best."

She flipped open her phone and checked the time. Ten hours, fifteen minutes, left. "I'll let you know tomorrow."

"As the apostle Matthew wrote, do not worry about tomorrow, miss, for tomorrow will care for itself."

"Yeah," she said, stretching her legs out and pushing the phone into the pocket of her jeans. "That's what I'm worried about."

Father Joe nodded, but Shelly was sure it was something he did when he didn't understand. She did the same thing in French class.

He turned and faced her. "I spoke with Father Tony last night. He said to me to say hello to you from him."

She clicked the end of her zipper with her thumbnail. "That's nice."

"Indeed, miss. Father Tony is a good and nice man. And he says hello to you."

"I got that, thanks."

"He also told me of the troubles that are vexing you."

The clicking got louder. "Like?"

The priest gestured with his hand, a little wave that implied nothing. Or everything.

"Funny. I thought what I said in confession was between me, the priest, and God."

"Of course, miss. Always. Father Tony would never violate the sacrament of confession. On pain of death. Of this I am sure."

"But he told you."

"Only what the counselors at the school had told him. The facts of the case, as they say on TV."

She swung her backpack onto her lap and yanked at the plastic snaps. "That's still more than he should have said."

"Miss. Please. I understand your distress."

Shelly glanced over at him and smirked. "Oh, *really?*"

"Yes, miss. I, too, have experience in this problem."

"You have no idea what you're talking about," she said as she dug through her backpack, rearranging the mess.

He nodded, but it was different this time. Then, slowly, he closed his eyes, drew in a long, noisy breath, and said, "I was nine when my twin brother died of malaria. His name was Samir."

Shelly stopped. "I'm sorry, I didn't —"

"My oldest cousin burned to death in a kitchen fire the same year. The following spring, we received word that my father had been killed by the Sudanese army. They thought he was with the rebels, but he was only a livery driver. They shot him anyway. With his death, we had to pay the cost of the vehicle. The strain was very hard on my mother. She had the AIDS and soon was too weak to work. When she died, my young sister and I lived with our auntie, and when Auntie died, we went to the orphanage run by the good Sisters of Mercy, thanks be to God."

Somewhere overhead, a ventilation fan switched on. Shelly listened as it ran through its cycle. When it switched off, the silence seemed louder than before. "It's not the same," she said, her voice quiet but firm.

"Miss, we have both buried members of our families —"

"That's not it, and you know it."

"Is it because I am from Africa and have seen many people die, so death is not as important?"

"No," she said. Then, louder, "No. That's not what I meant."

"What, then, did you mean, miss?"

"It's just not the same thing, okay? *God*," she said, growing louder, shaking her head. "What happened to you is horrible. *Unbelievably* horrible. But for me? It's different. That's all. Different."

"*My* brother died, *your* brother died . . . I don't see how it is so different —"

She spun around, grabbing a handful of his sleeve, twisting it, the priest pulled toward her. "It's different," she said, forcing the words out through clenched teeth, "because you didn't kill your brother."

The priest looked deep into her eyes.

She held his stare through her tears —

Held his sleeve in her fist —

Heard her own breathing, fast and uneven —

Felt his hand, warm and rough, press against hers

And through the storm in her head, she heard him say, "Neither did you."

She blinked.

"You did not kill your brother."

"Don't . . ."

"His name was Luke, and he was four months old. And he died."

"I killed him."

"No, miss."

"He's dead."

"Babies die, miss. This is the world we live in."

"No."

"So very sad."

"I was babysitting . . . he was crying . . . I put a blanket on him . . . and, and —"

"And you did nothing wrong."

"I was supposed to take care of him —"

"You did, miss."

"But the police took me away."

"Not to arrest you. To help you."

"They said they *knew* what happened."

"And they did. Everyone knew, miss. They knew you did nothing wrong."

"You're lying," she shouted, pushing him away, holding her backpack tight against her chest as she stood. "I *know* what happened. *I* put the blanket on him, and it *killed* him. *That's* why he died."

"No, miss, the doctors said —"

"*I killed him,* and that's why everyone hates me."

"No, miss. You are wrong —"

Shelly looked away. "I can't go back to being Marceli. I won't. You understand? I won't. I'm too close now. I have to keep it secret. I can do it."

"Miss, your family," Father Joe said, his voice rising to match hers, "they want to help you —"

"They hate me. They *have* to."

"No, miss. Your mother has tried so many times, but you —"

"Time," Shelly said, her eyes darting around the church. "There's still time. Yeah. Plenty of time. I can still stop it."

"Please, just relax, Miss Shelly."

"I can do this," she said, shouting now. "I can do it!"

She jumped up and ran down the long pew.

"Miss, *please,*" he said as he tried to follow, his shins bumping hard against the wooden bench, his long legs tangling in the narrow space. By the time he reached the carpeted aisle, she was gone.

TWENTY-SEVEN

FOR A THURSDAY MORNING, THE LIBRARY WAS CROWDED.

Eric leaned the chair back on two legs and looked across the lobby to the main entrance. His view was blocked by the desks and monitors and wires of the Internet station, and by the old people who shuffled from one computer to the next, wiggling the mouse until something they recognized popped up on the screen.

"She's not coming," Fatima said.

He angled to see the clock over the checkout desk. "It's only twenty after. Give her time."

"She's always the first one here."

"That just means she's late."

"What if she didn't get anything from her?"

"From who?"

"Katie. The girl she was gonna talk to," Fatima said. "The one I was supposed to punk."

"Yeah, what happened with that?"

"Nothing happened."

"If nothing happened, we wouldn't have met in Bullies Anonymous."

Fatima smiled. "Remember Annalise? She was a riot. I wonder what she's doing now."

"It was four days ago," he said. "I'm sure she's married with a couple of kids."

"*Four days?* That's *it?* God. Seems like forever."

"Don't worry. This time tomorrow it'll be all over."

"Our problems or our secrets?"

"We'll know in a minute," he said, nodding to Shelly as she cut around a woman trying to back her wheelchair down an aisle.

"Judging by the look on her face, it isn't going to be good."

Eric grunted something and dropped his chair forward, propping an elbow up on the table, resting his chin on his fist, trying to look relaxed.

"Sorry I'm late," Shelly said, pushing the glass door open with her hip. "Missed the bus."

"Don't worry about it," Fatima said. "You okay?"

"I'm fine," she said, and swung her backpack onto the table, randomly yanking open zippers as she sat.

Eric looked up at her. "Your eyes are all red."

Fatima kicked his leg under the table. "Want me to get you some water?"

"I *said* I'm fine. What did you find out from Connor?"

Fatima sighed. "Nothing important. He admitted to

bullying a girl at camp, but he wouldn't say who she was or what he did."

"And I got less outta Heather," Eric said. "She says she heard something about some girl getting picked on, but says that's all she knows."

"Her name," Shelly said without looking at them, holding up a screen-capture print of a tagged Facebook photo, "is Morgan Rouleau. And she was an assistant stage manager for *How to Succeed in Business Without Really Trying.*"

She looked over at Eric, then at Fatima—both of them eyes wide and mouths open. And five minutes later, when she was done telling them everything Katie had said, they still looked that way.

Eric shook it off first. "You knew this last night and you didn't think it was important enough to tell us?"

Shelly ignored his tone. "What would you have done if you knew?"

"Maybe I would have been able to fall asleep instead of lying awake all night," Eric said.

"Not me," Fatima said. "Knowing would have made it worse."

"So anyway," Shelly started, "Morgan Rouleau—"

"Ratted out her friends," Eric said. "She's nothing but a snitch."

"*What?* She did the right thing," Fatima said.

"It really wasn't any of her business," Shelly said, then shrugged, not sure if she agreed with herself.

"No way," Fatima said, her hijab flowing as she shook her head. "What they were doing was wrong. Period."

"Just because Islam says you can't do something—"

"Islam has nothing to do with this. It has to do with right and wrong."

"Exactly," Eric said. "And she was obviously wrong."

Shelly held up a hand. "It doesn't matter—"

"Yes it does," Fatima said. "This girl—what's her name? Morgan? She was *innocent.*"

"We all were," Shelly said, her voice changing. "But nobody stays that way forever."

It got quiet. Then Eric said, "We've got less than nine hours."

"Eight hours, twenty-four minutes, six seconds," Fatima said, glancing at her phone.

"We'd have more time," Eric said, nodding at Shelly. "If someone had shared what she knew—"

Shelly focused on shuffling her papers.

"—and right now all we know is this girl's name."

Shelly tapped the printout on the table. "And what she looks like."

Fatima studied the image. "Paste this under the definition of 'plain.'"

Eric slid the paper across the table. "What grade's she in?"

"She's homeschooled, but from what she says she's reading, she'd be a freshman."

"Okay, but that's still not enough to go on."

"The Internet is our friend, remember?" Shelly reached into her backpack and pulled out a small assignment notebook. "She lives at 1595 Town Line Road."

"Town Line? That's on the other side of the county."

"A minor detail."

"Says the girl who takes the bus everywhere."

"Her mother's name is Liz, and she works as an office coordinator for DJB Printing. I couldn't find anything about her father, but there's a Frank Rouleau who's about the right age living in Fairport, so maybe that's him."

"Or maybe not," Eric said.

"And check *this* out," Shelly said, tapping the page as she spoke. "Today is Morgan's birthday."

"Oh my god," Fatima said, "That explains *everything*."

"Not quite," Shelly said. "But at least it explains why it had to be today."

"Because every girl wants videos of people getting macaroni and cheese dumped on their heads for her birthday."

Shelly smiled at that. "The whole thing got started

when she wasn't invited to get high with the others on Connor's birthday."

"I don't think she wanted to get high," Fatima said.

"Sure," Eric said, drawing the word out. "It was this Connor kid's birthday, though. And now it's her birthday. I guess it makes sense in some stupid, drama-geek, drama-world way."

Shelly scribbled a line, then flipped the page to a bulleted list. "I haven't got everything worked out yet, but basically here's what we've gotta do. First we go to her house—"

"That's, like, thirty miles from here," Eric said.

"Good thing you have a car. Once there, we get her to invite us in—"

"No way," Fatima said, laughing as she said it. "I'm not going into that psycho's house. She could kill us or something."

"She's not going to hurt us," Shelly said.

"You don't know that for sure. Maybe she planned it this way all along. Right now she could be oiling up her chainsaw, just waiting for the bell to ring."

Eric raised his hand. "Question, Sherlock. She knows who we are and probably knows what we look like, right?"

"Yeah. So?"

"So we show up at her door, why would she let us in?"

"I'm working on that," Shelly said, writing another note, this one spilling over to the next page.

"It's all farmland out there," Eric said, remembering his ride in Garrett's car and his two-mile run. "What are we supposed to say, we were just in the neighborhood?"

"I said I was working on it. Geez."

"I don't see why we have to go in at all," Fatima said.

"Because that's where she has the evidence against us. And if we're going to get it back, we have to get inside."

"Oh, *I* get it," Eric said. "We're driving way out to Hicksville to force our way into the house of a girl we don't know—"

"We're not forcing our—"

"—and then stealing a few things. But it's not *really* stealing since it's our stuff to begin with."

"You make it sound so—"

"Criminal? I wonder why."

Fatima sighed. "I'm gonna be in *so* much trouble. Even if she doesn't chainsaw me."

Shelly started to say something, then folded her hands and set them on the table in front of her, closing her eyes and breathing slowly like Father Caudillo had taught her.

"Besides," Eric continued, "the thing she has on me? The picture? It's digital. It's on her computer."

"Me too," Fatima said. "She's got my books, but she scanned some of it. That's what she's gonna send out."

"No problem," he said. "When we're done stealing things, we can just smash her computer. I'm sure the police will understand."

They both looked at Shelly, who waited until it was quiet before opening her eyes. "Are you finished?"

"You don't think that's enough?"

"He's got a point," Fatima said.

Shelly nodded. "Everything he said is true. All we have is her name and her address. Assuming we can get out there — and assuming we can find the place — she's probably not going to let us in her house. And if she does, we're probably not going to be able to find your book or get at the computer files. And at nine o'clock, she's probably going to do exactly what she said she's going to do all along — send out emails to everybody we know, telling them the one thing we want to keep secret. And realistically? There's nothing we can do to stop her."

The silence lasted a full minute, then Fatima leaned in. "*But?*"

"But," Shelly said, "we're gonna try anyway."

Eric grunted a laugh. "We don't have a choice."

Shelly turned to a blank page and licked the tip of her pencil. "Okay, so you'll be driving, right?"

"I have a restricted license. I can't drive after dark."

Shelly looked at him. "So, you're driving, right?"

"Right."

Fatima scootched her chair closer. "How we getting in the house?"

Shelly smiled. "You ever read *The Odyssey*?"

"I saw the movie."

"Well, that's how we're getting in."

"What about my books?"

"I'm more worried about the computer," Eric said.

"Easy for you to say. They're not your books."

"If we can get to the computer, maybe we can delete the files. But don't expect me to do it," Shelly said. "I'm no computer expert."

Eric leaned back in his chair. "I know a guy," he said.

"And that means . . . what?"

"It means I know a guy who knows computers, that's all."

"So do I," Fatima said. "My cousin. But I'm not telling him anything."

"This guy," Eric said. "His name's Ian. He goes to my school. Kind of a loner. And a real freak. He's into all that computer stuff. I could tell him what we need — without giving him any details. He could tell us how to do it."

"Why would he help us?"

"Money."

"How much?"

"I don't know." He shrugged and thought about what he was supposed to have paid for the video work. "A couple hundred bucks, maybe more. You guys will have to chip in too."

Shelly nodded. "All right. Find out if this is something he can do and what it'll cost —"

"Wait a second," Fatima said. "What are you gonna ask him to do?"

Eric shrugged. "Wipe out her computer. Crash it. Something like that."

"No way," Fatima said, shaking her head. "We just want *our* stuff erased, that's all. Trust me, we don't want to piss off a computer geek."

"Don't be ridiculous," Eric said. "How's Ian supposed to know what he's looking for? He's gotta take it all down."

"If this guy's as good as you say he is, he can target specific files. I know *that* much."

"Why bother? If he wipes it all out, we'll be sure he gets our stuff."

"No, Fatima's right," Shelly said. "If we erase our stuff, that's one thing. She'll know it's over and she'll know not to mess with us anymore. But if we go after *her* stuff, that's like we're out for revenge or something."

"*So what?* She did it to us," Eric said.

"Check with this friend of yours," Shelly said, missing the look he was giving them. "See if he can take out *just* our files."

"And leave the rest of the computer alone," Fatima said.

Eric shook his head. "Whatever."

Fatima swiped on her phone. "We've got eight hours and twelve minutes. We won't have time to come up with another plan."

"Exactly," Shelly said. "And that's why we have to make sure this one works."

TWENTY-EIGHT

THE HOUSE WAS EMPTY, AND IT WOULD BE AT LEAST A couple of hours before his mother got home, but Eric moved quickly anyway, taking the stairs two at a time and running down the hall to his parents' bedroom. His iPhone was on the charging pad on top of the dresser, right where he knew it would be. He swiped it on, went to contacts, and scrolled down until he found the name and hit the call button. The phone rang eight times, and Eric was expecting it to go to voicemail when Ian said, "You owe me fifty bucks."

"I've been suspended. I'm back in school Monday — I can pay you then."

"Don't make me look for you," Ian said, then hung up.

Eric hit the call button again, and when he heard the click he said, "I've got another job for you."

There was a video game playing in the background, and after a burst of machine-gun fire, the sound dropped out. "Another cafeteria video?"

"No, this is different."

"Good. Because that was lame."

If it was so lame, Eric was tempted to ask, *why did it cost me fifty bucks?* Instead he said, "I need some files cleaned out of a computer."

"Clarify your terms."

"I need some files erased. Or deleted. Whichever is better."

"And by 'better' you mean . . . ?"

"Gone. Permanent. Forever."

"Obviously it's not your computer. You wouldn't need me to do that."

"No, it's somebody else's."

"Do you have it now?"

"No."

"When will you have it?"

"I won't. It's at her house."

"*Her* house," Ian said, a hint of twisted humor in his voice. "Interesting. Will you have access to this computer?"

"What kind of access?"

"Close enough to plug in a flash drive?"

"Maybe. But I doubt it."

"Which is it, Eric?"

He thought before answering. "No."

"That's too bad for you," Ian said. "The flash drive option would have been better. And by 'better' I mean cheaper."

Eric swallowed. "Can you still do it?"

"*I* can do it. But it'll take some cooperation on the part of your victim."

"I can't guarantee that."

"Neither can I. But I get paid whether she does or she doesn't. Now, when do you need it?"

Eric glanced at the clock and worked backwards. Thirty minutes to pick up the others, say an hour to get there, then ten minutes inside. "Four hours?"

"*Cha-ching.*"

"Is that a yes?"

Ian made a noise that might have been a laugh. "It's a yes to me adding on a one hundred percent rush fee. That's what you get for procrastinating."

"How much we talking?"

"Five," Ian said. "As in hundred."

"That's way too much."

"It'd cost more, but you get a return-customer discount."

"I don't know," Eric said. "It's a lot of money."

"Guess what? I don't care. You can take it or leave it. But if you want it, I need to know right now. Much to do on my end."

Eric drummed his fingers on the top of his parents' dresser, trying one more time to imagine a different option, a different way to get it done. Nothing.

He did the math.

Twelve bucks in his wallet and some cash in his room, maybe sixty bucks total, and another hundred or so on a debit card he could cash out. He could sell his phone fast enough, but that would raise way too many questions, so that left his Xbox games. He had the standard stuff, and nothing so new that it would be worth anything close to the original price. Even if he sold them all, he'd still be short, but with what Shelly and Fatima would kick in, it'd be enough. It had to be.

"Just so I'm clear," Eric said, "you're telling me you can make some sort of, what, virus?"

"You don't want to know."

"Okay. But whatever it is, it'll go in and just delete the files I tell you to delete. Right?"

"Right," Ian said. "All I'll need are the file names."

"What if I don't know the *exact* names?"

"Do you know when they were saved?"

"Well . . . yeah," Eric said, then a second later, "but . . ."

"Let me guess. Not the *exact* dates."

"No, not exactly."

"How about the month?"

Eric rubbed the top of his head as he remembered the day he had it all and threw it away. "June."

"Fine. It'll delete everything that was saved starting

June first, and anything that came after. Anything saved *before* that will be fine. Simple," Ian said. "For me anyway."

"What if it's a picture?"

"I *said* everything."

Hand on the back of his neck, phone to his ear, Eric paced his parents' bedroom.

It would work.

All their secrets cleaned out.

Erased like the whole thing never happened.

The picture — *that* picture — deleted, just like he had promised April.

It would work.

But it wouldn't be fair.

No payback for the shit she put them through, the way she played them, bullied them, yeah, even terrorized them.

No revenge.

No justice.

Just an end.

That's all Shelly and Fatima wanted, the only thing they needed.

But not him.

"I can hear you breathing, Eric," Ian said. "What's it gonna be? We gonna do this or what?"

Eric took a sharp, strong breath. "Can you delete it all?"

"Define, please."

"Can you get rid of everything on the computer? Every file, not just some specific ones. And every picture, too."

Ian hummed. "Nuked, huh?"

"That's what I want. Everything erased," Eric said, and after a pause he smiled. "And something added in."

"Interesting," Ian said. "Interesting and very doable."

"Then let's do it."

"Cash — no IOUs, no bullshit — paid in full before I show you what to do."

"No problem."

"And FYI, Eric. You screw me over on this, I unleash it on you."

"Don't worry, I'll pay."

"Oh, I know you will," Ian said. "One way or the other. Now let's talk about how this is going to work. And about this thing you want added in."

TWENTY-NINE

"You realize it's a school night, don't you?"

"Mom, I'm suspended," Fatima said. "I don't go back till Monday. Remember?"

"Please," her mother said, her hand, white with flour, touching her chest. "Some things I will never forget."

Fatima watched as her mother scooped balls of cookie dough onto the baking sheet, her sister Alya popping up at her side to swipe a finger along the edge of the bowl.

The clock over the stove read 4:50.

They'd be there any minute to pick her up.

Eric had wanted to come later, around seven, and he'd wanted to pick her up first, since Shelly's house was on the way to Town Line Road. But Fatima made it clear that if they wanted her along, she had to be out of the house before her father got home, and also, when the car pulled up and her mother looked out the front window, the only person she'd better see was Shelly, sitting in the driver's seat.

She had told Eric all of this when he called.

He didn't like it.

She told him she wasn't crazy about it either, but that's the way it had to be.

He told her he wasn't allowed to let anyone else drive his car.

She promised not to tell.

He doubted that Shelly had a license.

She said she was sure Shelly didn't, but that didn't change anything.

Then he sighed and asked her where she lived.

Her mother squeezed in another row of cookie-dough balls. "Did you help your brother with his algebra?"

"I don't need any help," Haytham said from the table.

"And what about your homework?"

"All done," Fatima said. It wasn't, but it wouldn't take long, and even if they asked to see it, she knew she could show them something that would pass for a week's worth of assignments. Her mother spent the next five minutes silently pinching and aligning the dollops, sneaking sideways glances at her eldest child. Then she wiped her hands and picked up the baking sheet, motioning for Fatima to come around the counter and open the oven door.

Fatima knew the silence, knew that her mother was trying to make her squirm, looking for any sign of nervousness that would hint at some devious plan. She was nervous and there was a plan, but there was too much riding on it to let it show.

Her mother adjusted the tray twice before standing to check the dials on the oven. "Who is this girl again?"

Fatima smiled. If it was going to be no, her mother wouldn't bother going through it all a second time. "Her name is Morgan," she said, staying close to the truth. "She's in this drama group after school. She got picked on really bad over the summer, and now she's got, like, no friends."

"And you have to see her tonight. Why can't you do this on Saturday?"

"Saturday's the car wash at the mosque. We're raising money for the Red Cross. I told you about that weeks ago. Besides, today's her birthday and we thought it would be nice if we dropped by her house to celebrate."

"Who is 'we'?"

The first lie was the hardest. "Just Shelly and me."

"Where does this girl live?"

The second came easier. "Close to school."

"And how are you getting there?"

The third rolled out on its own. "Shelly's driving. She has a car."

"You know I don't like you riding around like that."

"We're not riding around. We're going straight to her house and straight back home. I promise."

"How old is she?"

"Shelly? She's going to be eighteen," Fatima said, not counting it as a lie since it would be true eventually.

"No. The birthday girl. How old is she today?"

She picked a number. "Sixteen."

"And what did you get her?"

"Huh?"

"For her birthday. What did you buy her?"

Fatima's mind went blank.

"That's why you want to go, isn't it? Her birthday?"

"Yeah," Fatima said, scrambling to think of something, anything.

"So what did you get for her?"

"A book."

Her mother smiled and shook her head. "Why am I not surprised?"

"I guess I like books."

"Yes, and you like to write all over them. In the margins, between lines," her mother said, her finger scribbling imaginary notes in the air. "I can always tell when *you've* read a book."

Fatima faked a grin.

"But don't ever let me see you make a mark in a Quran," her mother said, the scribbling finger now underscoring every word.

"Mom, please," Fatima said. "I would never do anything bad like that."

Her mother hugged her. "I just want you to be a good girl."

Good like what? Fatima thought. *Faithful? Obedient? Unquestioning? Irrational? Doubt free?*

"*Insha'Allah,*" Fatima said, hugging back.

If God wills it.

THIRTY

ERIC SPUN THE WHEEL SHARP TO THE LEFT, SPLITTING
the yellow lines and stopping an inch in front of the guard
rail that separated pavement from the grass surrounding
the baseball diamond. He looked over at Shelly.

"*That's* how you pull into a parking space."

Shelly rolled her eyes.

"I thought you told me you could drive," Eric said.

"I thought I could. Besides, it's not like I hit anything."

"She's right," Fatima said from the back seat. "She came
close, but she didn't actually make contact."

"She drove from Walgreens to your house and back. It
wasn't even a mile."

"Fine, I can't drive, but I can count," Shelly said, holding up the small stack of bills. "And we're short."

"Impossible," Eric said. "I put in three hundred and
eight, and Fatima put in fifty-something—"

"Fifty-six, to be exact."

"Okay, that's what? Three sixty-four. And you said you
could get one-fifty—"

"No, I said I could get *close* to one-fifty."

Eric looked at her. "How close?"

"Eighty-one."

"Eighty-one?" He slapped both hands down on the steering wheel. "That's nowhere near close."

"What it is," Fatima said, "is fifty-five dollars short."

"This guy wants five hundred," Eric said. "We can't be short."

Shelly shrugged. "There's nothing we can do about it now. We'll just have to tell him that that's all we've got. We'll have to owe him the rest."

"It doesn't work that way."

"Shouting doesn't make it any better," Fatima said. "Maybe we can negotiate with him, get a better deal."

"With *Ian*? No way. He finds out we don't have the money — *all* the money — that's it, we're screwed."

"It's not like he'd come after us —"

"Yes, he would. He's a major freak. Going after people is what he does." Eric's left arm snapped out, his knuckles thudding against the padded armrest. "Count it again."

"It's not going to change."

"Maybe some bills got stuck together. Just count it, all right?"

Shelly thumbed through the bills, Fatima counting along over her shoulder.

"Four forty-five."

Eric rubbed a hand over his face.

No one spoke for a minute, then Fatima said, "Let's just go."

"Where?"

"The girl's house."

"And do what?"

"Ask her not to do it."

"You're crazy."

"No, listen," Fatima said. "Maybe that's all we have to do: ask her politely not to do it. Maybe she'll understand."

"I don't think so."

"We can try," Fatima said. "Or we can think of something on the way."

"We've got an hour and a half," Shelly said. "We're out of time to think of anything else."

"Oh, perfect," Eric said as he watched a black F150 pull into the parking lot. "Here he is now."

Fatima spun around in the seat, craning her neck to follow the truck as it crawled past. "A pickup? Seriously?"

"What did you expect, a Prius?"

The truck stopped, backed into a space fifty feet away, the shotgun rack impossible to miss in the rear window. Then the driver climbed out.

Fatima and Shelly stared.

"*Wallah*."

"*He's* your computer expert?"

Eric checked. "Yeah, that's Ian. Why?"

"'Cuz he's *hot*," Fatima said.

Eyebrows raised, Eric turned in his seat. "He's a freak."

"He's freakin' hot."

Eric looked at Ian as he strolled toward the car. Shaggy hair, rumpled shirt, open, with the sleeves rolled up to show off a pair of Japanese-style tattoos, a black and silver concert T-shirt underneath, skinny jeans, flip-flops. And yet they stared. It had to be a girl thing. He took a deep breath, then rolled down the window. "Hey."

Ian bent down, resting his arm on the roof. "Eric. Ladies."

Eric swallowed. "Did you get it done?"

"Of course," Ian said, smiling at Shelly as he spoke. "The phantom website, the password ignition, the names." He looked at Eric, nodding so slightly that it would be easy to miss. "Everything we discussed."

Fatima pulled herself forward. "What about the cloud?"

Ian grinned, shifting to look at her. "Forced login capture, remote delete, and account deactivation."

"And after?"

"Automated double-redundant backdoor sweep."

"Frequency?"

"Twice a minute. Two minutes would be plenty, but it'll run for ten."

"And it'll get the files Eric told you about, right?"

"It'll get what Eric is paying for."

Fatima nodded. "Nice."

Ian nodded with her. "Thanks."

Eric checked the dashboard clock and took another deep breath. "Ian, about the —"

"Nice shirt," Shelly said, leaning around Eric, pointing at Ian's chest. "Komor Kommando? Good stuff."

Ian looked down, tugging at the bottom of his shirt as if noticing the silver words for the first time. Then he looked back up, his smile shifting to a bullshit smirk. "You sayin' you've actually *heard* of them?"

"Not them," Shelly said, a laugh in her voice the others had never heard before. "Him. Komor used to be with Zombie Girl, and then Squarehead. But I like his solo stuff best. Especially *Das Oontz*."

Eric glared at her. "We've got —"

"It reminds me of first-gen KMFDM," Ian said, ignoring Eric, eyes locked on Shelly's.

"Then you should definitely check out the new stuff from Studio-X."

It took a moment, but the tribal connection clicked, all the unsaid things said with a smile and a nod. "Cool."

Shelly smiled back, then blinked and looked down at the money on her lap. "So, *anyway*. We've got your money."

Ian took a folded paper from his back pocket and held it out. "And I've got your solution."

"We're short," Shelly said. From the back seat, she heard a groan, and she could feel Eric's eyes burning into the side of her head.

Ian inched back the papers. "How much?"

"Two hundred."

"That's all you got? Two hundred bucks?"

"*Noooo*. We've got three hundred. But you said five, so we're short."

Ian looked at Eric. "Didn't I say to bring *all* of it?"

"You did. It's just that —"

"It's my fault," Shelly said, looking up at him. "I told these guys I'd have my share. And, really, I thought I would. I sold my necklace, but I didn't get as much as I thought. Eric put in more to cover for me, but it's still not enough."

He tapped the folded paper on the roof of the car. "I had a deal with Eric here —"

"So make a deal with me. I'll get you the rest. Just give me some time."

Ian brushed his hair back and looked at Shelly.

She didn't look away.

And when she saw his gray eyes soften, her whole body tingled.

"So you got three hundred, right?"

Fatima popped up. "Actually, it's —"

"Yup. Three hundred exactly." Shelly folded the pile of bills and held it out.

Ian reached in and tossed the paper on the dash, then put out his hand, palm up. "Close enough."

Shelly put the money in his hand, her fingers warm against his. "Thank you."

Ian wadded up the money and shoved it into his front pocket. "The instructions are pretty self-explanatory."

Eric unfolded the paper. "That's *it*?"

"You said you wanted simple."

"We do." Fatima read over Eric's shoulder. "But you could have been a little more specific."

"Trade secrets. I don't want to put myself out of business."

Eric flipped the paper over, checking to see if there was more on the back. There wasn't. "So we just do this and it'll all be gone?"

"It'll take a few minutes, but once it starts there'll be no stopping it."

"Perfect."

"And if it doesn't work, you get a full refund." Ian smiled a last time at Shelly, then headed back to his truck.

"Wait a second," Eric said. "You mean, after all this, it might not work?"

"It'll work," Ian said without turning. "But save your receipt, just in case."

THIRTY-ONE

THE GLOW FROM FATIMA'S PHONE TINTED THE INSIDE of the car blood red. Sound off, she watched as the digital numbers of the countdown clock clicked closer to zero. When she had first opened the email, there'd been more than forty-nine hours. Plenty of time. Now there was less than thirty minutes. Outside, farmland raced past, the glow of a crescent moon taking the edge off the late-September evening. On the seat next to her, a large pepperoni pizza steamed the back window. Up front, Shelly leaned over to check the speedometer.

"Can't you go any faster?"

"I'm doing fifty-two in a forty," Eric said.

"Just so you know, it's twenty-five of."

"And just so *you* know, we would have had a lot more time if we didn't have to stop off for pizza."

"We couldn't show up at her door empty-handed. We're there for her birthday, remember?"

"She's not gonna want any presents from us."

"It's not a present," Shelly said. "It's a prop."

"Our Trojan Horse," Fatima said, eyes still on the falling numbers.

Eric watched the road. "Wanna run through it again?"

"No," Shelly said. "We'll start confusing ourselves. Just stick to the plan."

Fatima looked up into the rearview mirror, catching Eric's eye. "Do you know how Ian set it up?"

"I'm the one who told him, remember?"

"Yeah, but how to make it run?"

"Yes, dear," he said.

"And not mess with her files?"

Eric grunted and looked away. "What, you think I'm stupid?"

"We'll see," Shelly said.

They rode in silence for five minutes, then from the dashboard, a woman's voice: "In one-half mile, turn left onto Town Line Road, U.S. Route two-fifty."

Fatima clicked her phone off. "I think I'm gonna puke."

Eric glanced in the rearview.

"Don't worry, it's just an expression. I'm really scared, that's all."

"Me too," Shelly said. "My leg's bouncing, and my heart's going like crazy. You'd think I slammed a six-pack of Red Bulls."

"We're almost there," Eric said, hitting the directional and braking for the turn, trying to keep his shaking hand on the wheel. "Just don't start freaking out and we'll be fine."

"What if she's not home? We didn't think about that," Fatima said. "Or what if we can't get in the house, what do we do then? We stand there with the pizza all night?"

"We'll worry about it then," Shelly said, the words snapping out. *"God."*

Eric looked over at her and smiled. "You saying a prayer for us?"

"Yeah, to Saint Jude. Patron saint of lost causes."

The woman's voice interrupted. "In three hundred yards, you have reached your destination."

Fatima leaned forward between the front seats. "I don't see anything."

"It's gotta be on your side. Nothing but fields over here."

"There it is," Eric said, slowing the car to a crawl, pointing to a low ranch-style house set far back from the road, no trees in the front yard, an SUV in the driveway, another on blocks at the side of the house. The porch was dark, but there were lights on inside. Eric spun the wheel, then hit the brakes and cut the engine, the car rocking to a stop behind the parked SUV.

Then no one moved.

Shelly took a deep breath. "Guys, I want you to know that if this doesn't work . . ."

"Same here," Eric said. "Let's go."

"Hold on a sec," Fatima said, then she reached under

her chin and worked the white cloth free, unwrapping the hijab in one fluid motion, her hair—a black jumble of waves and curls—falling to her shoulders. In the front seat, Shelly and Eric tried not to stare.

"You're staring," Fatima said.

Eric wanted to smile but didn't know if he should. "I thought you weren't supposed to take that off."

"Don't be ridiculous. I take it off every day." She shook her head and used her fingers to fluff up the flat parts. "Besides, they see an Arab-looking girl with a headscarf walking up to their house with a box in the dark, they're not opening the door."

"All people aren't like that," Shelly said.

"Maybe not," Fatima said, opening her door. "But I'm not taking that risk."

Eric carried the pizza, Fatima held the six-pack of Diet Cherry Coke, and Shelly rang the doorbell.

From inside they heard a shouted "I'll get it," then the door opened and a woman looked at them through the screen.

Shelly took a half step forward. "Hi, we're here to see Morgan."

The woman kept looking, but there was something uncomfortable about the way her eyes shifted, how her head tilted to the side as she turned the handle and inched open the door. "She didn't mention anything about people stopping by."

"It's sort of a surprise," Shelly said. "For her birthday?"

"Yes, her birthday," the woman said, the words coming out slow, as if she was piecing them together for the first time.

Eric held up the box. "We brought pizza. Pepperoni. It's her favorite."

"It's a bit late for a school night . . ." She paused, and they held their breath. "But I suppose you can say hello," the woman said, swinging the screen door wide and leaning away as, one by one, they entered.

Back at the Pizza Hut, they had filled the time waiting for the to-go order with predictions of what it would look like inside Morgan's house.

"I bet it's trashed," Eric had said. "Like one of those Hoarders Anonymous shows. Boxes everywhere, newspapers, just a path between the piles of junk."

"Cats," Shelly had said, shivering. "Lots and lots of cats. And that cat-pee smell. And fur. On everything."

"Dark," Fatima had said. "The kind of place you lure people to before you cut off their heads with a chainsaw."

Now, as they stepped in, they saw how wrong they had been.

The living room was bright and neat, with low, modern

furniture and a shiny, dust-free hardwood floor. Three Japanese prints — a mountain, a waterfall, and an orchid — hung on the main wall. To the side, on a teak-and-glass table, a muted PBS documentary played on a paper-thin flatscreen, and on the floor by the chair, a thick novel was bookmarked with a red ribbon. The house smelled like spring.

The woman shut the door behind them. "I'll tell Morgan you're here," she said, and disappeared down the hallway.

Shelly looked at the art, at the shelf lined with books, into the spotless kitchen with its overhead rack of gourmet pots and pans, glass-fronted cabinets, and granite counter-top, and thought of the place she was forced to call home.

Eric leaned over to Fatima. "Are you sure we've got the right Morgan?"

They heard a muffled knock and some mumbled words, then two sets of footsteps coming back toward the room.

"Smile," Shelly said. "It's showtime." And a second later the woman was back, and right behind her, wide-eyed and hesitant, the girl in the tagged Facebook photo.

"Surprise," Shelly and Fatima said in tandem, sugar sweet and giddy.

"Happy Birthday, Morgan," Eric said, trying not to look menacing.

"We brought pizza —"

"*Pepperoni* pizza," Eric said, going off script, his smile even bigger.

"—instead of a cake. Hope that's okay."

"And Diet Cherry Coke," Fatima said, holding up the six-pack. "Your favorite."

They stood there, grinning, holding out their offering, waiting for the eruption.

It seemed to take forever.

Stunned silence.

A blank stare.

Then slow recognition.

Realization.

A flash of terror in her eyes.

Her lip twitching.

A shaky breath, drawn in for a terrified scream.

Then a different kind of silence.

A different stare.

Thinking.

Connecting.

Assessing.

A second realization.

A gasp.

Eyes narrowing, the stare changing.

A flicker, then a gleam.

Lip twisting into a knowing smile.

Then Morgan Rouleau screamed.

THIRTY-TWO

"**O**H MY GOD, I DON'T BELIEVE IT, *HOW* DID YOU *KNOW*? YOU guys are *the best!*"

Morgan's smile slid into a smirk as she looked at each of them in turn, their blank stares fueling her energy. "Mom, these are three of my *best* friends from theater camp. This is—"

"I'm Shelly," she said, too loud, racing the words out, cutting Morgan off. "Shelly Meyer."

"Oh, I *know* your name," Morgan said, looking straight at Shelly. "She goes to St. Anne's."

Shelly pressed her thumbnail into the side of her finger and kept grinning.

"This is Eric Hamilton. He takes *really* good pictures."

Eric forced a smile. "Hello."

"And this is Fatima El-Rafie, who I *almost* didn't recognize without her headscarf." She tilted her head a bit as she looked at Fatima. "I thought you weren't allowed to take that off in public?"

"No, it's allowed," Fatima said, her olive cheeks reddening as she absently touched her hair.

Morgan turned to her mother, her hands pressed. "Is

it okay if we have the pizza in my room? I want to show them three projects I've been working on. We won't make a mess, I promise."

Her mother eyed the group, not bothering to hide her suspicions.

"Come on, Mom. I never have *anyone* over."

"I know," her mother said, a subtle warning not meant for her daughter. "Twenty minutes. Then they have to go."

"Thanks, Mom. Come on, guys," Morgan said as she turned, leading the way down to the last door on the left.

It was a bedroom like any other — bed, dresser, lamp, closet, posters, desk, a couple of chairs, computer — with a light blue and white color scheme and enough perfume bottles, stuffed animals, hair ties, bracelets, gum wrappers, and black-covered novels to link it to a ninth-grade girl. The EpicFail homepage was up on the screen, and in the background, Katy Perry sang about a road less traveled. Morgan spun the desk chair around and sat down.

"Just so you know, one sound from me and my mother will be in here in less than a second," Morgan said. "And she'll be bringing a gun."

They laughed, and Eric said, "A gun?"

"You want me to prove it?"

They stopped laughing. "Don't worry. That's not why we're here."

"Okay, then why *are* you here?"

Eric set the pizza on the edge of the desk, knocked a paperback off a chair, and sat down. "It's your birthday."

Her eyes narrowed.

"And because we did what we had to do."

"And we videoed it," Fatima said.

Shelly met Morgan's stare. "And we put it on YouTube. And now we're here to collect."

Eyes on Shelly, Morgan shifted in her chair, pulling the wireless keyboard onto her lap. "Give me the title."

"Not yet," Shelly said, and the way she said it — cool and low — made Eric smile. "We've got some questions. How'd you find us?"

She typed, and the generic YouTube homepage popped up on the screen. "If you don't tell me, I'm sending out your secrets."

"You said we had until nine. We still got a few minutes."

"Why should I tell you?"

"You tell how you found us," Shelly said, sitting on the edge of the bed, "and we'll tell how we found you."

Morgan looked at the screen. "I don't care how you —"

"Oh, come on," Shelly said, a whiny disappointment in her voice Eric and Fatima hadn't expected. "Aren't you even curious? It wasn't hard to figure it out. It *had* to be a lot harder to find us. We just want to know how you did it."

Morgan typed something, then backspaced it out and

paused. Then she said, "All right. Fine. But you go first. How'd you know each other?"

"We didn't," Eric said. "We met at an antibully thing we got sent to. You brought us together."

Morgan shook her head, punching the top of her thigh. She mumbled something, took a breath, and shrugged it off. "How'd you find me?"

The three of them looked at each other. Shelly nodded to Fatima. "Go ahead, tell her."

"The only thing Connor, Heather, and Katie had in common was that theater program," Fatima said. "When they told us what they did to you, we figured you were the caller."

Morgan tried to hide her surprise. "What did they tell you?"

"Enough to figure out who was calling."

Eric pointed at a microphone headset on the desk. "Is that what you used to change your voice?"

"That and some program I downloaded. It was easy."

"And so was finding you," Shelly said. "Now your turn."

Morgan leaned back and crossed her arms. "I needed somebody in their schools."

"We figured that much out. How'd you know about us?"

"You mean about all your little secrets?" Morgan waited, glancing at each of them in turn, but they didn't say anything, and a second later her swagger returned. "Everybody's got something to hide. *Everybody*."

"Maybe," Shelly said. "But you went after us."

"I didn't go after you, I *found* you." She smiled at Eric. "You're the one who gave me the idea."

Shelly and Fatima looked at him. Eric shook his head. "I've never seen you before."

"There was a football game at the school near here. Your school against that one. I went to see if I could spot Connor. I was planning on some sort of . . . accident. But I didn't see him. Not his sort of thing, I guess."

"How'd I give you the idea?"

Morgan's flat smile returned. "It was your phone."

"You took my phone?"

"I *found* your phone. I was watching for Connor from below the stands, and I saw it on the ground." She smirked. "Must have fallen out of your pocket."

"It couldn't have even been there two minutes," Eric said. "That's the first place I looked."

"It was way longer than that. Besides, I turned it in, didn't I?"

"After you went through it."

"Oh, and you wouldn't? All I did was swipe it on. It was already in the camera app, so I flipped through your pictures. Big deal."

"You shouldn't have done it."

Morgan looked at him, her smile growing, her voice dropping. "And you shouldn't have taken that picture."

"I guess you were in the right place at the right time," Shelly said. "But I don't see how that would give you the idea."

"Take a theater class," Morgan said. "Not acting, that's for posers. Backstage, that's where the fun is. Building sets, doing the lighting, props, sound effects — everything that makes a show seem real. You'll learn how easy it is to get people to do what you want if you set it up right. And I wanted to set up those three. But I knew I couldn't do it myself. If they saw me coming, they'd figure I was going to do something to them. And they'd be right. I wouldn't be able to get close enough. I had to find the right actors. When I saw the picture on Eric's phone, I knew I'd found *his* character's motivation."

"You knew you could threaten him with it to get even with Connor."

"Not just Connor. All three of them. The whole plan came to me in a *second*," she said, snapping her fingers, talking faster now. "How I'd do it, what I'd have to get. Everything. Starting with finding two more actors." She smiled at Fatima. "You were next."

Fatima swallowed hard.

"Your school, anyway," Morgan said. "I knew that that's where Katie went, and I knew that I had to have somebody there if my plan was going to work. It's close to the mall, so I told my mother I wanted to go shopping. She dropped me off, I cut through the parking lot to the soccer fields, walked right in, and started looking."

"For another lost phone?"

"I assumed I wouldn't be that lucky. I just needed something that somebody wouldn't want me to have. So I went locker fishing. Lots of open lockers. I got a whole bunch of stuff — love notes, cheat sheets, books, some pictures." She glanced at Eric. "None like *your* picture though, just things like drinking or normal making out, one that showed these stoners with a big bong."

Shelly said, "Why didn't you 'cast' one of them?"

"I tried," Morgan said. "The first one was a senior. She wrote this steamy love note to another girl. Lots of details. I called and told her I had the letter and that I'd send it to everybody at her school. She just laughed, told me to go ahead, that she didn't care what people thought. Then I called this other kid. He had these multiple-choice test answers written on the edge of a dictionary, but he barely spoke English, so I didn't call him back. Then I called you."

"Great, thanks."

"If it was anybody else, I don't think it would have worked," Morgan said. "I mean, who cares what you believe. Then I saw your name and figured you were an Islamic —"

"A Muslim," Fatima said.

"Whatevs. I read some of the stuff you wrote in the book, which was still no biggie, but then there were these notes like 'I could never tell my parents' and 'They'd be so upset if they read this.' It was perfect, like you wrote a script for me."

Fatima looked away, her hair falling across her face.

"Then there was your address book—how stupid was that? Every page was *filled* with stuff. You should watch what you write down."

"It's a shame you didn't try that at my school," Shelly said, grabbing a soda, clicking it open with one hand, playing it cooler than she felt. "Everybody knows everybody. You would've got caught in a second."

Morgan paused, her icy smile growing. "You *still* don't recognize me, do you?"

Shelly looked at the others, then back at Morgan, not sure who she was talking to.

"I shouldn't be surprised," Morgan said. "You were a year ahead of me."

Shelly blinked.

"Come on, think," Morgan said. "It wasn't *that* long ago."

"Wait, hold on," Shelly said, stalling, forcing her mind back, then, when it clicked, forcing the words out slow. "You went to Lockport High?"

"No. We moved here over the summer. Now I'm homeschooled. But two years ago, I was in middle school with you. You remember middle school, don't you? You should—you were one of the popular girls."

"I was *never* a popular girl," Shelly said, controlling her voice, keeping her nerves steady.

"More popular than me. At least, you didn't get picked on as much. Anyway, that was ages ago, right?"

"Right, so just—"

"But I still recognized you," Morgan said. "As soon as I saw you on the St. Anne's Facebook page. I was looking for Heather, and all of a sudden there you were, in a picture of new students. Your hair is different. It used to be light brown and she parted it on the other side, and it wasn't all wild like now," she said to Fatima. "Plus, she never wore that much eye makeup in eighth grade. But I knew it was her."

"Okay, fine," Shelly said, careful not to meet Fatima's gaze. "Let's get to the videos and get this—"

"So I looked for your name under the picture—"

Shelly motioned at Eric without turning. "Tell her the YouTube title or whatever it's called."

"—but it wasn't *your* name. I thought it was a typo. So I found another picture—"

"We get it," Shelly said. "Eric, tell her what to look up. We gotta get going."

Morgan looked into Shelly's eyes. "And that's when I knew I'd found the person I was looking for. Somebody with a secret *so* big she had to change her name and hide."

Shelly squeezed her fists tight, her thumbnails digging in.

"And your secret? It's absolutely horrible," Morgan said. "Whatever it is."

Shelly froze.

"I mean, it's gotta be something awful, right? Why else would you go through all that trouble?"

Sitting on the bed, Shelly watched as her knees started to shake, all of them staring at her, wondering.

"It was like you were pulling some witness-protection-program thing, only you're the criminal," Morgan said. "I searched you on Google, but nothing came up. It didn't matter, though. You never asked me what I knew."

Shelly felt faint.

"Whatever your secret is, you were willing to do some crazy shit to keep it hidden."

A white-noise roar filled Shelly's head.

"And that's all I needed anyway."

The noise grew louder as the meaning of Morgan's words sank in.

"Good thing for me you didn't ask," Morgan said, turning back to the keyboard, the YouTube homepage on the screen. "No more delays. What do I type?"

Eric glanced at Shelly, her eyes glazed over. "Mac and Cheese Punks Three," he said, sticking to the script, then leaned back and watched the screen. Morgan typed the words and hit ENTER. A page-long list of videos popped up. The first two were paid ads, and all but one looked like cooking shows.

Eric scooted his chair forward and looked down the list, remembering his lines. "I don't see it," he said.

"If this is some kind of —"

"Just hold on," he said, faking the irritation in his voice. He pointed to a red screen capture he'd had Ian post two hours ago. "Try that one."

Morgan clicked on the image, and a standard YouTube page appeared, and in the player, a red screen, the white words were easy to read:

**THIS VIDEO HAS BEEN DEEMED
INAPPROPRIATE AND REMOVED.**

Eric punched the air. "That's *bullshit,*" he said, then turned to Fatima. "I *told* you we should have waited."

"I'll tell you what sounds like bullshit," Morgan said, her smile gone.

"You think I'm lying? You think I didn't post the videos?"

"I don't think you did *any* of it. None of you. You showed up here, trying to fake your way out —"

Eric pulled Ian's note from his pocket and tossed it on the keyboard. "Try this."

Morgan looked at the paper, then at each of them.

Her eyes narrowed, and she smiled as she typed.

She hit ENTER and the screen went white, the little circle on the tab bar spinning as the browser loaded.

The webpage appeared — silver accents on a black background with a white rectangle space that said "password."

Morgan raised an eyebrow. "Well?"

"Secrets," Eric said. "All lowercase."

Morgan typed the password and hit ENTER.

The page refreshed, and there were six white squares in two even rows, just like he had described to Ian. Centered in each square was a black play arrow, and above that, a name.

"The three you want are on the bottom," Eric said, his finger tapping the squares that read KATIE, CONNOR, and HEATHER. "Click on one of them and it'll play."

Morgan hesitated, her hard grin twisting as she ran the cursor over the top row, buying it. "What about this Lisa one? What's that about? Or these two that say 'Bianca'?"

"They're nothing. These are the three you wanted."

"Videos?" Morgan smiled at Eric. "I thought you would have learned your lesson." She moved her hand, and the cursor slid down, centering on KATIE.

The word turned light blue.

Morgan's finger twitched.

Click.

A warning box appeared on the screen.

Morgan clicked "Download anyway," and it disappeared.

Another box came up, this one with a stop sign.

She clicked "Proceed."

A progress bar popped up in its place, the red line inching up the scale. They watched as it moved across the screen, holding at 87 percent forever, then flashing ahead to 100 percent, where it froze.

A muffled rooster crowed, and they looked at Fatima. She pulled out her cell phone and hit the mute. On the screen, the countdown clock was all zeros. Then they jumped at the knock, Shelly gasping as the door flew open, Morgan's mother scowling from the hallway. "Two minutes," she said, then pulled the door shut with a thud.

Shelly set the near-full Coke on the desk. "We're outta here."

Morgan looked back at the screen. "This isn't playing."

"They're big files. It'll take a while," Eric said. "It'll play."

"It better."

"And then you delete all the stuff you have on us. *Everything.*"

"I told you I would, and I will. Once I get these videos up on YouTube."

"And don't ever try contacting any of us again. For anything. You do, and I swear we'll call the cops."

"The same goes for you," Morgan says.

Fatima coughed. "Can I have my books back now? I don't want to have to come all the way back to get them later."

"I didn't want you here in the first place," Morgan said, then opened the desk drawer and took out a worn, yellow-covered book. A spiral address book was jammed between the marked-up pages. "I have scans of all the good parts, anyway."

Fatima took the book and slid it under her arm, front cover down, and out of habit mumbled a thanks as they crossed the room.

Shelly opened the door, half expecting Morgan's mother to stumble in, but the hallway was empty, and from the other side of the house she could hear the faint strains of a TV theme song. "Let's go."

Eric and Fatima followed her out, and the three of them started down the hall, Morgan a step behind, glancing over her shoulder. "This better work."

Eric looked ahead at Fatima and Shelly, then back at Morgan. "You're right."

THIRTY-THREE

THE VOICE ON HIS IPHONE SAID, "I KNOW YOUR SECRET."

He paused, took a breath. "Really?"

"I think so," Fatima said. "Does it have something to do with a picture of you dressed up like SpongeBob at a Halloween party?"

Eric laughed. "Where'd you find that?"

"Something you said the other day at Starbucks got me thinking. So, is that it?"

He started to say one thing, then said, "No, it's a little worse than that."

"What, Mr. Krabs? Patrick the starfish?"

"Why is this so important to you?"

"Because you know my secret, so I should know yours."

"I didn't ask, you just told me."

"I wanted you to know. I didn't want you thinking it was something horrible."

"I never did."

"Yeah, right," she said.

"What if it is?"

"Is what?"

"Horrible. What if my secret is something really bad? Would you still want to know?"

She was quiet for a moment. In the background he could hear her kid sister singing along with a Disney movie. "No, I guess not."

Eric exhaled. "It was a picture I took of a friend. If people we knew saw it, my friend would have been really embarrassed."

"It wasn't even of *you?*"

"No, just . . . my friend."

"So you went through all of this to keep someone else from being embarrassed?"

He closed his eyes and lied. "Yeah, I guess."

"That's sweet," she said. "You're a really good friend."

"Thanks," he said without thinking, the expression she couldn't see saying how he really felt.

"Speaking of friends, have you heard from Shelly?"

"I haven't talked to her since I dropped her off that night."

"Me neither. I told her to call me. I figured we'd keep in touch or something, but I guess not," Fatima said, a second later adding, "She's kinda weird."

He grunted.

"Ever find out who she really is?"

"She said her name was Shelly," Eric said. "That's good enough for me."

"I wonder what she did that was so bad."

Eric shook his head. "I don't want to know."

"You think she hooked up with Ian?"

He pictured them side by side, Ian and Shelly. Same dark clothes, same shaggy black hair, same bizarre T-shirts, same haunted stares. The perfect postapocalyptic, cyber-goth, techno-loving, hard-style couple. "Maybe."

"As weird as she is," Fatima said, "if it wasn't for her, we never would have met."

"No. If it wasn't for *Morgan,* we never would have met."

"Actually," Fatima said, adding an exaggerated Egyptian accent. "If I didn't scribble notes on everything and if you didn't take embarrassing pictures of your friends . . ." She laughed, then said, "I'm just glad it's over."

It took him an instant to replay it all in his head.

The phone call.

That voice.

Lying awake, staring at the ceiling, his stomach one big knot, scared shitless.

Then — everything.

What he had done to Connor.

To his parents.

To April.

And Morgan.

At least there was that.

Shelly and Fatima didn't have to know everything.

Whatever.

He was just glad it was over.

There was no way he could go through that again.

THIRTY-FOUR

"**Thank you tenfold for facilitating such a thun**-derous participation from the worshipers."

Shelly smiled with the priest. "There were twenty people at the mass. I wouldn't call it thunderous."

"You were not standing at the pulpit, miss. When I said 'God is good' and they shouted it back, the rafters shook with joy."

"Maybe the church needs a new roof."

"Mr. Nacca told me how you stood at the front door of the church and asked all who entered to participate fully," Father Joe said. "Thank you for that kindness."

Shelly shrugged, her cheeks reddening as she looked away. Father Joe straightened a stack of hymnals at the end of the pew.

"It's good to see you happy, miss."

"Happier, anyway," she said, still smiling.

"And do you know the source of this great happiness?"

She thought of Ian's late-night phone calls, hanging out at Sips Coffee and listening to Komor on his Beats headphones. But she kept that to herself. "There's this girl at my school," she said. "I was sort of, well, mean to her. Anyway, this week I finally had a chance to apologize. She was actually cool about the whole thing."

The priest nodded. "Forgiveness is a great blessing. This is why we ask God to forgive us as we forgive others." He paused and looked into her eyes. "And why we must forgive ourselves."

"Now you sound like Father Caudillo."

"I consider that a fine compliment, miss. And he is right." Father Joe sat next to her, his long, bony fingers intertwined on his lap. "You need to forgive yourself for what happened to your brother."

"I know I'm supposed to," she said, not wanting to cry, yet knowing it would happen anyway. "But it's hard."

"People ask me, 'Why does God let innocent babies die?' and I have to tell them that I have no answer. Crib death — that is what we call SIDS in Sudan — it is a tragedy." He paused. "And a test of faith."

"Don't worry, my faith is fine. It's my patience that gets tested." She sighed and brushed the back of her hand across her cheek. "Everybody looking at me. Whispering about me. Like I can't guess what they're saying."

"Perhaps it is not what you think."

"I need some time, that's all. I mean, I close my eyes and I'm right there, like it just happened, like he's still —"

She took a deep breath, letting it out in choppy bursts, then another, the nausea fading. "I just don't need people reminding me about it right now."

Father Joe smiled and rubbed his hands together, finishing with a clap that echoed through the empty church. "As you wish, Miss Shelly. I shall not mention it again. When you are ready to talk, we will talk. Till then, I will pray for you, and I will pray that others respect your privacy."

Shelly smiled. "Sounds like a plan."

THIRTY-FIVE

SHE TOOK TWO PAPERS OUT OF THE THICK MANILA folder.

She had the file saved on her new laptop, but that was just one of the mistakes she wasn't going to make again. Besides, there was something about seeing her handwritten notes mixed in with typed pages that made it all seem more personal. Maybe that girl Fatima wasn't so stupid after all.

The first paper was a list of names and numbers.

It had taken weeks to come up with a fresh list, then twice as many weeks to narrow it down. There were several excellent candidates for the role, but she knew now that the more actors you had on stage, the more that could go wrong. They'd start comparing notes, changing the plot, conspiring against the director, ruining everything.

Best to clear the stage, recast the lead, and start from scratch.

This time there'd only be one.

And nothing would go wrong.

She'd make sure of that.

She popped the top of a yellow highlighter and circled a new name.

The second paper was a printout of the only thing that had survived on her old computer.

A photo.

Maybe he was trying to be ironic, but she doubted he was that deep.

The iPhone camera flash in the bathroom mirror whited out his face, but it spotlighted Eric Hamilton's fist, middle finger raised.

She slipped on the headphones and adjusted the mike.

She opened the effects program on her laptop, selected presets, and clicked on one.

She checked the number by the circled name and dialed.

An unsuspecting actor about to make a shocking debut.

The phone rang a dozen times before a shaky voice said hello.

She paused, listening to the clicking pops, the airy whoosh, letting the static build.

Eric thought his troubles were over?

They were just getting started.

Acknowledgments

Thanks to —
Anne and Patty, for the brilliant calls.
Dinah, for picking up on the first ring.
Molly and Laurel, for not hanging up.
My family and friends,
for not losing my number.
Some Ska Band, for the party line.
Librarians, teachers, and booksellers,
for never phoning it in.